Messenger of Doom

One stern-looking woman stepped off the boardwalk. "Those men need medical attention. Aren't you going to do anything?"

Slocum pushed in close and cut Booth's hand loose from the horn. Then he shoved him out of the saddle, and Booth fell to the ground with a scream. He simply lay there.

"Why I never—" the woman protested.

"Listen, they rode into Mrs. Branch's place last night shooting real bullets at where they thought we were sleeping. Ma'am, they'd've not even sent flowers to our funerals if we died. Now, you can fix them up or let them die. I don't care. Send word to Yates. Let him tend them. They're his hired hands."

"What's your name, mister?"

"Slocum." He looked over the hard-eyed crowd of women, children, and men. "Tell Yates I said he better not try anything else, or I'll bring his carcass in here for the buzzards to pick his eyes out."

DON'T MISS THESE
ALL-ACTION WESTERN SERIES
FROM THE BERKLEY PUBLISHING GROUP

THE GUNSMITH by J. R. Roberts
Clint Adams was a legend among lawmen, outlaws, and
ladies. They called him . . . the Gunsmith.

LONGARM by Tabor Evans
The popular long-running series about Deputy U.S. Marshal
Custis Long—his life, his loves, his fight for justice.

SLOCUM by Jake Logan
Today's longest-running action Western. John Slocum rides a
deadly trail of hot blood and cold steel.

BUSHWHACKERS by B. J. Lanagan
An action-packed series by the creators of Longarm! The rous-
ing adventures of the most brutal gang of cutthroats ever as-
sembled—Quantrill's Raiders.

DIAMONDBACK by Guy Brewer
Dex Yancey is Diamondback, a Southern gentleman turned con
man when his brother cheats him out of the family fortune.
Ladies love him. Gamblers hate him. But nobody pulls one
over on Dex . . .

WILDGUN by Jack Hanson
The blazing adventures of mountain man Will Barlow—
from the creators of Longarm!

TEXAS TRACKER by Tom Calhoun
J.T. Law: the most relentless—and dangerous—manhunter
in all Texas. Where sheriffs and posses fail, he's the best man
to bring in the most vicious outlaws—for a price.

JAKE LOGAN

SLOCUM
AND THE
FOUR PEAKS RANGE WAR

J

JOVE BOOKS, NEW YORK

THE BERKLEY PUBLISHING GROUP
Published by the Penguin Group
Penguin Group (USA) Inc.
375 Hudson Street, New York, New York 10014, USA
Penguin Group (Canada), 90 Eglinton Avenue East, Suite 700, Toronto, Ontario M4P 2Y3, Canada
(a division of Pearson Penguin Canada Inc.)
Penguin Books Ltd., 80 Strand, London WC2R 0RL, England
Penguin Group Ireland, 25 St. Stephen's Green, Dublin 2, Ireland (a division of Penguin Books Ltd.)
Penguin Group (Australia), 250 Camberwell Road, Camberwell, Victoria 3124, Australia
(a division of Pearson Australia Group Pty. Ltd.)
Penguin Books India Pvt. Ltd., 11 Community Centre, Panchsheel Park, New Delhi—110 017, India
Penguin Group (NZ), 67 Apollo Drive, Rosedale, North Shore 0632, New Zealand
(a division of Pearson New Zealand Ltd.)
Penguin Books (South Africa) (Pty.) Ltd., 24 Sturdee Avenue, Rosebank, Johannesburg 2196,
South Africa

Penguin Books Ltd., Registered Offices: 80 Strand, London WC2R 0RL, England

This is a work of fiction. Names, characters, places, and incidents either are the product of the author's imagination or are used fictitiously, and any resemblance to actual persons, living or dead, business establishments, events, or locales is entirely coincidental.

SLOCUM AND THE FOUR PEAKS RANGE WAR

A Jove Book / published by arrangement with the author

PRINTING HISTORY
Jove edition / December 2009

Copyright © 2009 by Penguin Group (USA) Inc.
Cover illustration by Sergio Giovine.

ISBN: 978-0-515-14722-3

JOVE®
Jove Books are published by The Berkley Publishing Group,
a division of Penguin Group (USA) Inc.
375 Hudson Street, New York, New York 10014.
JOVE® is a registered trademark of Penguin Group (USA) Inc.
The "J" design is a trademark of Penguin Group (USA) Inc.

PRINTED IN THE UNITED STATES OF AMERICA

10 9 8 7 6 5 4 3 2 1

PROLOGUE

Amy Branch looked up from shaving thin strips of meat off the beef hindquarter to catch sight of her dun horse looking downhill at something. Beads of sweat ran down her face as she set the knife aside, wiped her bloody hand on her apron, and quickly picked up the the Navy model Colt off the table. She used a flour sack to mop her wet face one-handed, but didn't worry about all the blood from butchering splattered on the too-big man's shirt and old canvas pants held up by the galluses on her shoulders.

Who in the hell was coming? In her early thirties, Amy ran the 7C Ranch, at least what was left of it. Her husband, Ernie, was doing two years in Yuma on a trumped-up charge they called horse stealing. Ernie never took nothing wasn't his—*sonsabitches* anyway. But the Bar O owner wanted his patented land and water, and when Ernie wouldn't sell it to him, Old Man Yates cooked up the scheme to move him out. They were all in on it. Sheriff Roger Cummings and his bunch of cronies, and Alvin Yates, who owned the Bar O— she hated that man—and the judge, Horatio Dugan, who they bought off. But Yates wasn't getting this place. She walked over to the edge of the ramada so she could see the rider when he got into sight. Better not be none of Old Man Yates's crew. She'd blow him to hell and gone.

"Howdy, ma'am," the rider said, and swept off his hat with the sweat-stained band.

"Howdy yourself." She didn't know this man, who was in his twenties. By his dusty clothing, he looked like a drifting cowhand, but he was a long ways off the main road and must have been told how to find her.

"What's your business up here?" she asked.

"I'm out of a job. Fellow in Oxbow said you might need some help." He sat his jaded horse and looked around.

"What fellow in Oxbow?"

He shook his head. "Never said his name, just mentioned that Mrs. Branch might need a ranch hand. You are Mrs. Branch?"

She nodded, tight-lipped. Was this some trick of Yates? Was he some drifter the old man had hired to infiltrate her ranch and learn what she was up to?

"Where do you hail from?" she asked.

"Texas. I was raised down on the Lampass. My name's Kyle Moody."

"Mine's Amy Branch. Who've you worked for?"

"Mrs. Branch, nice to meet ya. Been to Kansas twice with Big John Duncan's herds. Thought I'd see New Mexico. Never found a ranch over there needed help, and I've been on the chuck line ever since I left there. Don't seem like anyone needs a cowboy these days."

"I could use one, but the pay'd be thin till I sell some cattle in the fall. I ain't got no fancy ranch house." She slapped the post of the palm-frond ramada. "This is headquarters, and you better not mind taking orders from a woman."

"I reckon that's no problem." He dismounted heavily, undid his cinch, stood the saddle on the horn and wet blankets on top, then sent his weary horse off toward the large stone tank.

Was he real, or Old Man Yates's plant? She could worry about that later. She had beef to jerk before the flies got to it.

"Wash your hands." She pointed to a pan and pitcher. "I don't know if you ever made jerky, but that's what we're doing today."

"Show me the way."

In a short while, he was busy slicing strips off across the table from her. She was hanging them on her rack, and the pungent mesquite smoke was covering them under her makeshift canvas tent. He sure wasn't acting afraid of woman's work.

"When was the last time you ate a meal?" she asked.

"Two days ago."

"Why didn't you say something?" She frowned at him.

"I asked ya for work. I figured you'd get around to food sometime."

She closed her left eye and studied him in the shade of the ramada. "I guess you did need work. I'll fix something. I bought this quarter of beef off Nick Thomas this morning. We'll have us some steaks off of it and biscuits. I can see we'll have plenty of jerky."

"Anything else that you need me to do, Mrs. Branch?"

"There's some firewood in a stack over there. Bust me up some that'll fit in that sheet-iron stove."

"Yes, ma'am."

She admired his hatchet ass as he moved across to the pile of dry branches and dead trees she'd snaked in behind her horse. It was obvious he'd been ranch-raised and knew how to work. My heavens, she hadn't had a lick of help since they'd sent Ernie off in that prison wagon to Yuma. Been six months since she'd had him in her blankets, and it would be another year and a half before her man even got out.

Her eyes squeezed tight at the thought of being that long without a man. Ernie better come home horny as a billy goat because by then she'd either really need him or have forgotten all about doing it.

After she washed her hands, she cut off several thin steaks. They'd cook fast and would be more tender than thick ones. Then she went to making a batch of sourdough, folding the liquor in the mound of flour on the dry sink. Soon, she was cutting biscuits with a large whiskey jigger and had them ready. She greased the Dutch oven with the hot coals under it and put her bread in it, then placed on the cast iron lid with a shovel of red-hot coals to top it.

Kyle brought her an armload of wood, and she stoked up the fire under the large skillet. She melted beef tallow in it, and soon had it boiling hot. She dredged the meat in a flour, salt, and pepper mixture and set the pieces in to fry. Her latest hand sat on his haunches at the edge of the ramada puffing on a roll-your-own. The aroma of the smoke made her want one—but she'd never smoked.

She poured him a cup of coffee and asked if he used sugar and cream. He shook his head and rose. "Thanks, my teeth were about to flood out smelling that joe boiling."

With a nod, she went back to check on her biscuits. Satisfied they'd soon be done, she walked to the stove and turned over some of the browned meat with a long-handle fork. Be nice to share a meal with human being—it had been a while.

They put the supper on their laps and ate sitting crosslegged on her large Navajo rug. The last of the sunset faded in the west as she tasted the rich food. Kyle seemed like a hundred other good men she'd known in her lifetime. She felt she was home again in the panhandle of Texas, in a family cow camp with her brothers and cousins, eating chickenfried steak and steamy hot biscuits. Shame the two of them didn't have some fiddle music.

Then, without warning, six men with guns drawn and flour-sack masks appeared out of the night. She shared a shocked look with Kyle. Her heart sank.

"Make a move for a gun and you're both dead."

Then they walked in, and one bashed Kyle's head with a pistol butt. He sprawled out face-first on the ground. Amy's heart stopped. These men were nothing short of vicious animals.

"Get her undressed."

His words drew goose bumps over the skin on her shoulders and the backs of her arms. They were powerful men that she couldn't push away, and they soon tore off her shirt and then jerked her boots and pants away despite her kicking and swearing at them through her teeth.

Then they painfully pinned her down on the blanket. She looked up in disbelief at the leader when he dropped his pants to his knees and knelt down with his horse-size cock ready in his hand.

"Nooooo!" she screamed.

1

Slocum got the letter, which had been forwarded many times, in Magdalena, New Mexico. He nodded thanks to the postal clerk, who remarked, "You must sure move around a lot."

With a laugh, Slocum walked out on the porch of the post office and opened the letter postmarked Oxbow, Arizona Territory.

Dear Slocum,

I didn't know if this would find you but I sure need your help. They railroaded Ernie on a trumped-up horse-stealing charge to two years in prison. Old Man Yates and his outfit want the ranch and the water but I'm not giving it to them. They killed a young man I hired to help me the night he showed up, and in the same visit they took turns using me for a pin cushion. I don't need to tell you that part. They all wore masks, and of course the damn law said there was nothing they could do about it since I had no names of the gang members.

Please come if you can help me. Lord, I know you

7

*have enough problems of your own. I won't stay at the
home place anymore, not after what they did to me, but
I'll keep a lookout for your arrival.*

*Best
Amy Branch*

"That bad news?" Abe Brown asked, sitting on his good
roan horse and holding the cap of his horn in his palm.

"Bad enough."

Abe Brown was in his sixties, tough as twisted barb wire,
and ran lots of cattle up on the New Mexico-Arizona line. He
spat tobacco off the far side of the stout red roan horse, wiped
his mouth on the back of his sun-scarred hand. "Whatcha got
to do?"

"I guess, with your cattle here at the railhead and sold, I'll
head for Arizona and see if I can help some old friends."

"Hell, I was planning on us having an elk hunt come fall
up near Mount Baldy."

"Hate to spoil your plans, but I better go see if I can help
my friends. Soundcd pretty rough from this." He waved the
letter.

Abe scrubbed his face with his hand. "Get that saddle off.
I'm a giving you Christmas early."

"What are you talking about?"

"I'm sending you off on old Red here. I figure you're
planning on making some tracks to wherever this is, and
Red's got more bottom than that horse of yours."

"You don't have to do that."

"Listen, I'm near sixty winters old. I know exactly what
I've got to do and don't have to do, too." He stepped down so
Slocum could uncinch his saddle. Then Abe fished a roll of
bills out of his vest pocket. "And take this, too."

"That's too much." Slocum looked at the wad of money in
his palm.

Abe reached up, stuffed the bills in Slocum's vest pocket,
and gave him a shove. "Now get going."

"I'm going, Abe, quick as I can." He carried Abe's saddle around and tossed it on his former horse, a big bay.

"Lord, son, we've had a great summer together up in them White Mountains. Cattle sold well down here. Seems like ever since I paid that bank note off, the market's been good to me."

"Tell the crew thanks for me."

"I will, and you remember you've always got a roof and food to eat at my place. *Via con Dios, mi amigo.*"

"Same to you, old man. Thanks for Red, too." Then Slocum reined Red around and left in a lope.

Slocum crossed lots of country. He swung north to avoid the great chasm of the Salt River and came in off the Mongollon Rim through Tonto Basin, then dropped south to Rye Creek. A store, post office, blacksmith shop, and a saloon, plus some corrals used to gather stock for drives, made up the sparse settlement on the high banks over the dry wash christened as Oxbow.

He bought some grain for his horse at the store and then, with a feed sack hung on Red's muzzle, Slocum crossed the dusty street to the Irish Saloon. The place was dark inside and stank of a million spilled beers and drinks, sour sweat, and tobacco: Both traces of smoke and the smell of chewing tobacco remained in the air.

"What'll it be, stranger?"

"Good whiskey."

The man behind the mustache nodded. "I have some."

He produced a bottle and a glass.

Slocum nodded. "Pour me a double shot to cut some of this trail dust out of my throat—"

Some heavy boots clunked in with loud Mexican rowels strapped on them. A tall man filled the double batwing doors. "Whose gawdamn roan is out here at the rack?"

For a moment, Slocum considered the whiskey in the glass and then the man in the doorway's reflection in the mirror over the back bar. "I never saw your name on that hitch rail."

"Who in the hell are you?"

Slocum turned slowly, satisfied that his .44 was on his hip and would not be any trouble to draw and fire if the situation called for it. "I'm the man owns the roan horse."

"What's your business here anyway?"

"Mister, your manners are atrocious. I don't have to tell you one damn thing except you keep on, you maybe will end up in a pine box."

"Gunslinger, huh?"

"No."

The man drew a deep breath and looked ready to explode.

In a slow wave, Slocum spread his left hand out toward the man to halt him. "Now, if you take one more step toward me, you better have a funeral suit."

"Why, you—" The man blinked in shock, looking at the cocked .44 in Slocum's right fist.

"Now just go outside and go about your business. My name and my business and my roan horse are none of yours, friend. And by the way, drop that gun that's in your holster on the floor real easy before you leave. The man behind the bar will have it for you later."

The red-faced man started to protest, then must have thought better and obeyed, but Slocum could see his shoulders under his shirt shake in pure anger when he bent down to place it on the floor using his fingertips to hold the grips. The hinges on the batwing doors creaked swinging back and forth for a few seconds after his departure. Slocum walked over and recovered the Colt. It was new and oily-smelling. He emptied the cartridges one by one on the bar, and then slid the revolver over to the bartender.

"Who is he?" Slocum asked

"Yonken. He's Old Man Yates's ramrod. He thinks he owns Oxbow. You better not turn your back on him."

Slocum nodded and looked over the low curtains in the window at the street out front. The man was out of sight. "Here, I haven't paid you for the whiskey."

"Hellfire, you don't owe me nothing. Seeing you run

Yonken off was worth the whole damn bottle. My name's Tommy Burke."

"Mine's Slocum." They shook hands across the bar. Slocum drank his measure of liquor, then turned down the offer of more, nodded thanks to his newfound friend, and headed outside.

He halted on the shaded porch and stood for a moment to let his eyes become accustomed to the bright sunlight outside. Then he ducked under the high rack and undid the reins. The skin on the back of his neck itched when he vaulted into the saddle. Be a good place to be shot at from ambush. He set Red in a short lope and left Oxbow.

Ernie Branch's place was lower down under Four Peaks Mountain. It was giant saguaro and prickly cholla country. There was something everywhere to stick a spine in a man. He took the wagon road southward, thinking he could recognize the cutoff that went east to the ranch. Tough country to ranch in, but Ernie liked it. Slocum'd bet he sure wasn't liking Yuma prison. No one needed to poll the man either— Slocum knew that for a fact. Ernie had been framed by his enemies for a crime he didn't commit, and incarceration was a bitter pill to swallow for an innocent man.

It was late afternoon when he came up the dry wash and could see the pole corrals and palm-frond ramada on the rise. The hot wind was flapping a flaglike towel hanging in the shade.

He dismounted, pulled the pants and chaps out of his crotch, and stretched his tired back muscles. Not much sign of life around there. Maybe if he built a fire in the sheet-iron stove, she might see the smoke and come in.

He carried some roasted coffee beans in his saddlebags. He squatted before the stove and began making a fire. With plenty of busted firewood handy, he soon had the blaze going and rose stiffly. No sign of anyone or anything. The towering heights of the Four Peaks rose above him, and a few vultures rode the hot wind, kiting around in search of a meal. Some topknot quail whit-wooed in the brush, and doves around the tank called to their mates. Saguaros and chaparral were all around him, and there were a few noisy wrens.

He unsaddled Red and carried his saddle and blankets over to the shade. When his kac was resting on the horn, he squatted down and watched Red roll on his back in the loose sand. Then the gelding rose and shook a dust storm loose. The cow pony had a good habit of sticking around Slocum, so he didn't hobble him, and that let Red go get himself a drink from the rock tank and then graze around on the dry bunchgrass.

Satisfied he had to wait for Amy to find him, he put on coffee water and fed more wood to the fire. Not a cloud in the sky. He mopped his wet face on his kerchief and sat cross-legged on a faded Navajo rug under the palm-frond roof. The hot breeze felt cooling.

He was about to consider a nap when he heard the water begin to boil, and he went to add the crushed beans to the pot. He'd no more than dumped them in when he noticed Red looking back toward the wash Slocum had ridden up on. In seconds, he had the .44/40 out of the scabbard and had knelt down looking for visitors through the iron sights.

He saw a white-bearded man under a floppy hat riding a burro and leading two more burros loaded with packs.

"Whoa, Joshua!" The man bailed off his old army saddle and looked at Slocum, who'd risen and walked to the edge of the ramada.

"Where's Amy? Mrs. Branch?" the man asked, licking his sun-scarred lips.

"They ain't here right now."

"Well, I know why *he* ain't here. Yates and them rascals railroaded poor Ernie, but-but the Missus—she all right?"

"My name's Slocum. I'm an old friend and I came down here from Socorro when I got the word. I just got here. But she told me in her letter it might not be safe for her to stay here."

"Goldang that Yates outfit. She's a wonderful lady and

them messing with her makes me mad enough, if I was a young man, I'd go over there and clean their plow."

Slocum nodded. "I know how you feel, pard."

"I'm going to water my burros, but I'll be back to jaw with you in a short while."

"My coffee will be made by then."

"Thanks for offering me some." The old man waded off, leading his animals toward the tank.

Slocum would have to find out his name when he came back. The hills were full of those old boys looking for fortunes and not finding many. They dry-panned enough gold flecks for supplies, or got someone to bankroll them on another search for the big one. Optimists all of them, but most were square shooters. This old man looked and sounded sure enough like a good one.

Later, he told Slocum his name was Rufus McClain and he'd prospected from Canada to Mexico. Found a few good ones, but they petered out. Through the rest of the evening and their supper of frijoles, Rufus told him about prospecting. After sundown, Rufus finally went off to a place across the wash where he'd parked his things, and left the ramada to Slocum.

A coyote went to yipping when the moon came up. Some mustang stallion challenged anyone in camp when he, his mares, and some colts came into the tank for water. Red rambled down to the ramada, and Slocum went out to pat him on the neck.

"Kinda bossy, ain't he?" Slocum asked his horse, and waited with Red till the mustangs had their fill and left. By then, the gelding was standing hipshot and asleep. Slocum used a blanket to wrap in, and dozed lying on the Navajo rug. By morning, when all the desert heat would be evaporated, it would be chilly.

He awoke in the night to the soft ring of a spur rowel, and someone squatted beside him. An Apache Indian could not have come up that quietly. With a big yawn, he released his fingers from the revolver under the covers and stretched.

"Getting in kinda late, ain'tcha?" he asked.

"Took you long enough to get my letter," Amy said, squatted on her boot heels beside him.

"Got it a week ago in Magdalena. It had been forwarded several times." He sat up and tried to shake the sleep from his brain.

"Yeah, I mailed six of them to try and find you."

"One did anyway. How are you?"

"Horrible—" She dropped on her knees and hugged him. "I swear to God, these last months have been the worst days of my life."

"Easy, easy," he said, holding her tighter as she began to sob. "Tell me the whole thing."

She straightened up back on her knees and flung tears aside. "No. You hold me. We can talk later. I just want you to hold me."

"Well, take off your boots and spurs and we'll get under this blanket. I've come to help you. Any way I can."

Ruefully shaking her head, she dropped on her butt, sniffling, and shed the footgear. Then she rose, shoved the galluses off her shoulder, and pushed her pants off. In the starlight, her shapely legs were encased in men's long underwear. Then she scrambled under the blanket he held open for her to join him.

With her hands clasped together in front of her, she snuggled up against him. "Damn, I figured you'd never come—"

"I'm here now." He raised her chin and kissed her. It was like kissing a dead woman's lips. Then her arms went up, encircled his neck, and she became alive and vibrant, her mouth and tongue hungrily attacking him for more.

His hands molded her pear-shaped breasts under the shirt and underwear. They were firm and neat to feel and weigh, and when he undid some buttons, they spilled out. With a start, she gasped out loud and pressed herself up against him. He moved down and grazed on them until her nipples turned to stone points. With her hugging him to them, he could hardly get his breath. But his mind was in a whirlpool of pleasure—who cared if he breathed or not?

She broke away for a moment and slung off the shirt. Then he helped peel her out of the long underwear. He'd shed his pants and when they rolled together again, the first touch of her smooth leg to his sent lightning to his brain. In a flash, she was underneath him and he was between her legs.

When he eased his throbbing erection into her, she cried out, "Yes, yes."

Fiercely, she hugged his head to her as he slowly drove past her ring and into the depths. Her bare heels beat a tattoo on the back of his legs. Raising her butt to meet him, she began to sling her head from side to side, and soon began moaning, lost in passion's waves. The wavelike contraction inside her tried to strip his aching dick as they sought each other's final curtain.

Then he came. Like a huge rocket blasting off to explode high in the sky and rain a shower of sparkles back to earth. At last, lying on their sides, face to face in each other's arms, she raised her leg, reinserting his cock inside her, and pressed tight together, they fell asleep.

2

Sitting on his butt beside Amy's sleeping form, Slocum could see across the wash. The old man had already left. No doubt he'd known that they obviously wanted to be alone. The sun had been up for a while. She reached up and pulled him back down with her.

"There ain't one damn thing needs to be done today—save you and me."

He lay back down with her. "Tell me about Ernie's trouble."

"He went down to Phoenix. Really to Hayden's Mill, to buy a wagonload of grain for the horses and get some supplies. Some fella offered to sell him a short-coupled blazed-face sorrel horse. Ernie didn't know the man, but he was buying that good-looking horse for me. So he paid him and the seller gave him a bill of sale. In a hurry to get home, he never tried to find a brand inspector. You know how hard they can be to find when you need one?

"So he hitched the sorrel on behind the wagon and drove home. He was a fine horse. I loved him and believed thirty bucks was less than half the price Ernie actually paid for him. But in a week or so, a deputy out of Globe and one from Phoenix were at our ramada wanting to know if we had a sorrel horse belonged to a Mr. Achers down at Tempe.

"Ernie told 'em no, but we had a sorrel horse that once belonged to C.K. Howard. They asked to see him, and he went and brought Baldy in. Well, of course, Baldy matched the brand inspection papers that they had.

"Why hadn't he followed the law and had him inspected? Ernie knew the law, but ordinarily when it isn't a trap, there isn't any problem. But there was no C.K. Howard to be found, nor has anyone answering his description been around down there.

"Ernie recalled the whole thing. How the fella rode up leading the sorrel and stopped him. Said he was from Lehigh and he was going down to sell the sorrel, cause he needed money for his wife's doctor bills."

"Anyone know him in Lehigh?" Slocum asked.

"No." She made a face, snuggled up to Slocum under the covers. "Not one sumbitch had seen this fella on the road or the bald-faced horse, but they all damn sure saw my husband leading him home.

"The jury found him guilty, of course, and lots of folks pleaded with the judge, but he still got two years. Old Man Yates gave the prosecutor a thousand dollars, the county sheriff five hundred, and the deputies got a hundred apiece as well. Folks said Yates was afraid of the judge."

"When did they rape you?"

She buried her face in his chest. "It's been six weeks, maybe two months ago. They caught me here alone with this new hand I'd just hired. They killed Moody in cold blood. Poor boy. Masked men. There were more than three—they wore flour-sack masks. I didn't know them. Two of them pinned me down and the leader, who did the talking, raped me first. Then a skinny kid, and another one I figured was young. I was so upset—I should have listened more. One of them they coaxed forever to rape me, but he wouldn't. Maybe he couldn't do it. That made four.

"I won't ever forget the leader's voice—those lousy bastards."

"Did they talk about anything?"

"Yeah, for me to get off this place or they'd be back to rape me again."

"Did you see anything you can remember?" he asked, hugging her.

She nodded her head until her bobbed hair was in her face and tears sparkled on her brown lashes. "I can recall lots of things. Some are too nasty to talk about. The first boy had a bad scar on his hip like a bull had gored him sometime. The other boy was freckled all over his body. Probably redheaded, and the one led them had a—corkscrew dick big as a horse's." She buried her face in Slocum's chest. "On his gun butt there was some kind of shiny medallion embedded in the redwood grips."

"Anything else?"

She shook her head.

"They weren't any of them cowboys from around here?"

"No. No, not around here that I knew. Hold me tight, Slocum. I hated that night so bad. I swore I'd never tell anyone again about it after that Deputy Scroggins from Globe told me I'd need their names to file charges."

"He wouldn't do nothing to investigate it?"

"Acted like it was my fault that I got raped. He suggested I move into town until my husband got out of prison. You know he's on Yates's payroll."

Slocum nodded. "I ran into Yates's headman, Yonken, yesterday. He was demanding to know who owned Red."

"That big bastard needs killing."

"He came close yesterday to being planted in boot hill."

"Oh, Slocum." She closed her eyes and her fingers fondled his privates. "Make me forget this nightmare."

So he obeyed her.

Slocum and Amy spent the next few days checking on her stock. In this harsh land, water holes were most important. A dried-up hole could send the cattle looking for new water, which meant they could move miles, and then contribute to overgrazing in the area adjacent to that new source of water. Slocum knew that in the desert, keeping cattle scattered over a range that could support them was critical. Amy carried along a small pick and trenching shovel on the packhorse to dig out any spring that was blocked.

They reached the Black Wash Tank in mid-morning, dismounted under the straggling cottonwood tree, and hitched their ponies.

"This the one needs to be mucked out?" he asked her, taking the shovel off the pack orse.

"I hate for you to have to do that," she said, dismounting.

"Won't be the first tank I've cleaned," he said, and began toeing off his boots.

"I'll cook us some lunch then if you'll do that."

"Sure," he said, hanging his pants on a mesquite, and then crossed over to the tank on bare feet. When he stepped into the long narrow tank, the warm water was well over knee deep, but the slurry of mud came up halfway to his knees. The long tank was made of mortar and rocks and had required many days to build, but held lots of water. Deep in the ravine, there wasn't room for a large round tank like the one Ernie'd set up at the ranch headquarters.

Shovel by shovel, he spaded out the sediment of slop. The mossy water turned a muddy color and his back muscles complained, but the muck from the bottom was being removed. If nothing was done, in time the water tank would have been full of the alluvial sand and clay that had washed in.

Amy busied herself building a fire and breaking up dead branches to feed it. No stranger to men's work, she could swing a short-handled ax one-handed. It was a shame selfish men like this Yates were so greedy for control of all the land that they'd separated her from her man in such an underhanded way. He tossed out another shovelful dripping in water, then went back for more. When he mopped his face on his sleeve, it was pushing noon, sun time, and he was half-way down the trough.

He put some more effort in it, and soon had the muck out. Then, rather than walking out in the spines and goat-head stickers, he waded up to where the spring spilled out a wooden chute into the tank. The clean water swirled in where he bent over and drank his fill. Cool sweet refreshment. No wonder Old Man Yates wanted this place. Ernie and Amy had developed water all over this country.

Some Sonora doves lighted in the dust, and began stalking around looking for any grain that had gone through a horse. He waded back down the trough to his clothes and boots, and she met him with a feed-sack towel to dry his legs and feet.

"You got that whipped out easy," she said.

"Wasn't easy." He shook his head, drying one foot, then the other, while seated on the wall. "It was pure hell."

He put his pants on, and then his socks and boots, then rose, bent over, and kissed her. His efforts caused a smug smile to cross her thin lips. With a knowing nod, he strapped on his six-gun and then guided her to the fire.

She bent over and lifted the coffeepot. "Ernie said when we came here we had to develop the water, then spread out only enough cattle that this land would support. Course he wanted feed left for those years when it didn't rain, too. Idiots like Yates run all they can and then some, and they're ruining their range."

"It'll come to haunt them."

"I think so, too. But with Ernie in jail and Yates set on taking over—" She chewed on her lower lip. Then, on impulse, she rushed in and tackled Slocum around the waist. "Damnit, Slocum, I know you've got worse things dogging your heels, but I need you in so many ways."

She looked up at him for an answer, and he nodded solemnly to reassure her. He knew and understood her problems, and he'd stay as long he could. They ate her lunch of reheated beans, coffee, and leftover biscuits.

After lunch, they packed up and started for Indian Wash.

They were crossing through some chaparral country with several paloverde trees dotting the flats when he heard something. He reined up and touched his lips.

"What is it?" she hissed.

"I heard a calf bawl."

"You sure?"

"It wasn't a momma-come-here bawl either. Stay here," he said, and jerked the Winchester out of the scabbard. In two jumps, Red was in a run, and they went down the dirt bank into the deep dry wash on his butt. He hit the loose sand and made a turn upstream.

Slocum saw them. The bawling calf was tied on the ground and its half-Hereford momma was having a fit, pawing dirt and bawling at its captors. Both startled-looking men went for their sidearms. Slocum rose in the saddle, took aim. Then with his first shot, he hit the one standing over the calf with the iron. The second man's horse tore loose, and the man threw up his hands.

"Don't move a muscle," Slocum ordered, swinging off Red to the ground with his smoking rifle ready. A quick check over his shoulder and he saw Amy and the packhorse coming off the bank after him.

"Who-who are you?" the boy in his late teens stammered.

"The man who's going to hang you for rustling cattle that don't belong to you."

The boy's jaw dropped. Slocum squatted down beside the one shot and moaning on the ground.

"Where are you hit?" Slocum asked.

The boy rolled over on his back. "I'm dying."

He looked younger than the one standing. In disgust, Slocum shook his head and set down the rifle. The blood on the side of the rustler's shirt looked like it was too far to the side to be a deadly wound. With both hands, Slocum ripped the shirt open, examined the wound, and saw the bullet had only grazed his ribs. Maybe broke one or two, but he'd live to see a judge.

"Know them?" Slocum asked Amy as she dismounted and ran up to join him.

"Albert brothers."

"Who do they work for?" Slocum asked.

"Don't know." With hands on her hips, she looked hard at the calf. "Who's damn brand did you put on him?"

"A one-oh-three brand," the one standing said.

"Who's that registered to?"

"We ain't sure."

"No, Nathan Albert, you know who owns that brand." She was right in his face.

"I swear—I swear."

"You better tell me or I'm going to brand *you*."

"A cow buyer named Drithers."

"You know him?" Slocum asked her.

She shook her head.

"Where did they come from?" Slocum asked.

"Their father ranches north of Oxbow."

"How much is Drithers paying you?" Slocum asked.

Nathan shrugged his thin shoulders. "Half of what they send him."

"What's that mean?" Amy asked with a puzzled look.

Slocum scowled, realizing what they were up to. "If that calf is sold somewhere, the owner of the brand gets the money. Brand inspection looks after that."

"I don't understand," she said, still looking confused.

"Whatever that calf would have brought at roundup. The money for him goes to the brand owner."

"So you could use a running iron on a critter and get paid for him. Damn, I guess I never knew that. We better patch Webb up so he can live to see the judge." She went to the packhorse for bandages.

Slocum untied the calf and it got up on wobbly legs. Then it galloped off after its mom, who left the dry wash in a hard run with her tail over her back, her calf keeping up.

The trip to Globe took the rest of that day and half the next one. When they arrived, Amy dropped out of the saddle, looking at the new courthouse. "I hate this damn place."

"So will *they*," Slocum said, indicating the Albert brothers.

"The law better do something with them." She took a deep breath, and then looked slit-eyed at Slocum. "If that deputy says one word—I'll kill him."

Then, in a low voice, she said, "I should have done that last time."

They marched the two rustlers up to the office marked SHERIFF, and a clerk looked up sharply when Slocum put their gun belts on the counter.

The clerk cleared his throat loud enough to wake the dead. Obviously, a signal to someone in the next office.

"What can I do for you today, Mrs. Branch?" the clerk asked, rehooking his glasses behind his ears and coming to the counter.

"We caught these two using a running iron on one of my calves," she said.

"Why, one of them has been shot—" The clerk looked aghast.

"Both of them ought to be hanged—where's Sheriff Cummings?"

"Right here, Mrs. Branch." The thickset man in his forties stood in the doorway dressed in a wrinkled brown business suit with a dirt-stained white shirt, his tie undone, and his pants stuck in his boot tops.

"We caught these two red-handed branding one of my calves with this running iron," Amy said. And she slammed it on the counter.

The sheriff took hold of his lapels and strode over to the counter, looking the Albert brothers over. "You two mistake a calf you thought was your daddy's, boys?"

"Yes, sir," Webb said, bent over, holding his side like it was killing him. "And he shot me for no reason at all."

"Tell the sheriff your partner's name," she insisted.

Webb swung around and almost straightened up, but acted like the pain had caught him. "We didn't have no partner."

"Sheriff." Slocum stepped up. "These so-called boys

weren't putting their daddy's brand on that calf. They were putting a one-oh-three on his hide for a man called Drithers."

Cummings blinked. "I don't know you. What're you saying?"

"My name's Slocum. I'm helping Mrs. Branch till her husband is pardoned."

"Pardoned?" Cummings put his hand to his mouth to cut off his amusement. Then he straightened his shoulders. "They ain't about to pardon Branch. He'll have to serve out all his time and more."

"We ain't here to talk to you about that. We're here to sign the papers on these two rustlers."

"Where do I know you from?" He squeezed his chin.

"You don't."

"Well, Mrs. Branch has been in here not a month ago claiming some masked men raped her. No names or descriptions. Now she's back with two innocent enough young boys and saying they were rustling her cattle." Cummings shook his head in disapproval.

"They were rustling cattle."

He turned up his hands. "It's your word against theirs, I'd say."

"Are you telling me that you aren't going to charge them with rustling?"

"Slocum! Slocum!" She was pulling on his sleeve. "We need to leave. I told you he might not do anything about them."

"Better listen to the lady. She's got some good advice."

"Wait," Slocum said to her, keeping his eye on Cummings all the time. "I want him to tell me in his own words he isn't going to proceed with this arrest."

Cummings swaggered over to the counter with his hands still clinging to his lapels, and spat out his words. "I damn sure ain't messing up two innocent boys' lives with your drummed-up charges."

"Good," Slocum said. "And we won't bother to bring any more in here. Cottonwood trees don't turn you away."

"You go to taking the law in your own hands, you'll find out what the law can do."

"Lot of steep canyons up there. A man could fall off his horse and break his neck. Be a shame if it happened to you."

"I could lock you up." Cummings's face was beet red.

"You could do lots of things. Looks to me like you've done enough for one day."

Amy had Slocum's arm, and dragged him out of the office. "We've got to go. They'll do you like they did Ernie. Come on. Come on."

At the hitch rack, Slocum looked back at the courthouse. He was fuming mad. He slipped in beside the bay that Webb rode and as unobtrusively as he could, cut the cinch in two. Then he did the same with Nathan's dun horse. Let the riders fall hard.

"Come on. Come on," she insisted.

He swung up on Red and nodded. "Damn waste, wasn't it. Well, you warned me. That sumbitch needs to be thrown out of office."

One more scowl at the new two-story stone building, and he shook his head, checking Red. Cummings had not seen the last of him.

3

"We better go hide in the cave," Amy said as they headed out of Globe. Repeatedly looking back over her shoulder like she thought the devil was after them, she trotted her horse hard.

"Cummings worries you, doesn't he?" Slocum asked from beside her.

"More than that. We haul in two rustlers and he says they are innocent boys and won't press charges." About to cry, she shook her head in distress.

"I agree that made me mad as hell, too."

"I didn't want you in jail, too." Tears began to stream down her cheeks. "This has been hell, Slocum. Damn poor hell."

"Hold up. They ain't following us." When she stopped, he rode in and hugged her. "We'll whip 'em. You'll see."

"But how? They're the law." A new river of tears ran down her face.

"Trust me. We may have to go to Prescott and see the governor before this is over, but we're going to settle it. Cummings and his cronies aren't that powerful."

"I sure hope we can do something. That back there was bad—innocent boys my butt. And I knew he'd hang a charge on you before I could get you out of there. I guess we'll have to den up in that cave for now."

"Whatever you think."

She nodded, and they short-loped their horses through the hills. By late evening, they were at the forks of the Salt River and Tonto Creek. They took the ferry, and Slocum talked to the ferryman, whose name was Luke, as they crossed the river.

"Guess you have lots of business up here?" Slocum asked.

The older man on the winch laughed. "No, sir. But it's a living for me and the kids. My wife died a few years ago and left me four young kids. She was twenty years younger than me and I sure miss her."

"I bet you do. Old Man Yates come through here often?"

"Sometimes. Oh, every few weeks."

"By himself?"

"Naw, he's usually got that Yonken with him. Big bully of a fella. Why do you ask?"

"Just curious."

"They framed her old man, didn't they?" He motioned toward Amy.

"Yes. How did you know?"

"Hell, everyone up here knew him. He never stole that horse. Yates wants all of the other ranchers out of that country. Larry Sisk said he told him to leave or die. I guess he's still up there, but afraid to leave his place or they'll burn it. He knows that worthless sheriff ain't going to do a thing."

Slocum nodded. "I just wanted to know."

Slocum and Amy rode off the barge and headed north. They made camp on Tonto Creek about dark.

"I say gnaw on some jerky and take a bath while we have the chance," she told him. "What do you say?" For the first time since they left the Gila County seat, she smiled at him. Hat on the back of her head with them standing in the shadow of the Mazatzal Mountain Range that towered over them, he'd figured it was a challenge and not a question.

"Lead the way," he said, on one knee while hobbling the last horse.

She slung her hat off and tossed it aside on the bedrolls and panniers. "I know what you want and I know what I want. And it ain't jerky, so I'm going bathing first. I want no complaints that I smell like a horse."

Slocum laughed, running behind her as she raced downhill for the stream under the cottonwoods. His boots dug in the loose sand of the embankment, and they hit the flat together, him toeing off boots and shedding clothes to meet her challenge. In the growing twilight he could see her pear-shaped breasts swinging as she fought off her clothing. He finished undressing ahead of her, and rushed out in the knee-deep cool water, then dove in to swim upstream.

Poor Ernie was cooking in that oven-hot prison at Yuma, and Slocum was up here with his lovely wife. Still, Slocum needed to get him out of prison and find a solution to this crap involving Cummings and Yates. Amy was a bonus for Slocum. He watched her in the dimming light dive in and swim to him. They both rose, and she half staggered into his arms. They kissed in water less than knee deep, and her rock-hard nipples dug into his chest. Their embrace stole his breath away, and sent an urgent message to his dick to stiffen.

She glanced down at the stick between them and laughed. "But I'm not clean yet."

"I grabbed a blanket coming down here," he said. "Those rocks under your back can be sharp."

"Oh—" She reached down and folded his erection against her belly, then moved in and kissed him. "I don't care—we can do that for a while and then swim and do it some more. I just want to forget this screwed-up life I'm trapped in."

"You're calling the shots."

"Let's go try him."

"He's willing."

With her long hand in his grasp, they crossed the swift stream and ran across the alluvial sand to the blanket. She flung it open and they kissed again. This time with more promise and growing anticipation of things to come. A quick drying with sack towels, and they were in each other's arms on the blanket. When he was between her knees, he rose up and inserted his aching cock in her gates, and gently pushed it in a series of probes past her ring of fire. She spread-eagled her legs for him. He braced himself over her, savoring the tightness and contractions that began inside her.

She raised her butt up each time to meet his thrust, and they were soon swirling into a whirlpool of fiery passion. Their hard-muscled bellies, lubricated by their sweat, rubbed on each other with each pounding. His efforts to bury himself inside her grew harder and faster. Her efforts to suck him inside her grew wilder and wilder.

Then, a sharp pain in his testicles signaled him to bury his throbbing dick in her and fire off his artillery. Her eyes became glazed over. She gasped hard for air with her mouth wide open, and when he exploded, she fainted.

Totally exhausted and spent, they lay in each other's arms and slept a few hours. When she began to pull hard on his tool, he awoke to see the sparkling stars in the sky. Her breasts swung over him as she straddled him, inserting his half-full erection in her cavity, and settled down to accept it.

He reached up and clutched her hips to help her ride him. She would have been nice to have gone along on Abe Brown's roundup during the past few months when he'd slept alone. These hot days were probably the last before fall came to the Mazatzal Mountains and Four Peaks.

He started to rise, and signaled that he wanted to be on top. She slipped off. With her underneath him, he could probe her harder and eventually get his gun off. The change went as he had planned and soon he eased himself into the saddle again. He closed his eyes and scented the night wind. The smell of the river, the sharpness of creosote from the brush, and her musk filled his nose. Filled with a deep need, he drove on and on, harder and harder, until they both exploded and he could feel her juices rush out and drown his balls.

Wrapped in the blanket against the growing night's chill, they clung to each other and fell back asleep. At dawn they dragged themselves out of their bed, saddled, loaded the packhorses, and ate jerky while climbing up through the pass and over the top.

By mid-morning, they were at the cave. It was high enough to be in the junipers and piñons, and the fresh turpentine smell was in the air as they dismounted at the mouth of the cave. The entrance yawned open like the mouth of some huge prehistoric animal under the wind-polished sandstone face. In this higher altitude, it would be lots colder than the chaparral country beneath them. The land rolled away in a long sweeping slide down through foothills to the Verde River some fifteen to twenty miles west of their location.

No doubt the Apaches had once used this range. Skeleton Cave, where many Indians were slaughtered by the army when they refused to surrender, was south on the Salt River. Anyone who came up there would either be lost or looking for Slocum and Amy. He used his brass telescope to scan the countryside after they had unloaded and the saddle horses were hobbled. A spring-fed tank was built under the cave opening, and the grass was plentiful up there, so the packhorse wouldn't leave.

There was an ancient cliff dwelling inside the rim, and that made it a defensible place if required. And anyone who charged across the open ground in front of the cave mouth would have to be a fool. He saw a trace of smoke to the north. Nothing else caught his eye in the spyglass. He'd need to kill a deer or a mountain sheep to supplement their larder. Plain frijoles got old after a while.

He went back to where she was arranging things. Seated on his butt, he noted the large supply of firewood—he wouldn't need to go after any of that right away.

"I wondered what you've been thinking," she said, looking back at him as she bent over, browning some coffee beans in a skillet over her fire.

"We need to make a sweep of all the water holes, then light out for Prescott and see the governor."

"Sounds good, but you know it's a hard ride, two, even three days up there over some damn rough country."

"You ain't up to it?"

She rose and shook the hair out of her face with her back turned away from him and the shapely butt encased in those canvas pants staring back at him. "I guess we can do it."

"Hell, girl, there ain't much we can't do."

"Could we bust Ernie out of jail?"

"I understand you miss him, but if we can get the governor's ear, we might do that, too."

"I'd like that."

"We'll work on it."

She turned and grinned big at him. "It ain't that you aren't the best man in bed. I just miss him a lot."

"Hey, I ain't taking his place. I'm just filling in." They both laughed aloud.

Before dawn, when the Gambel's quail scurried around under the bushes, he took his rifle and scope and went hunting for mountain sheep. He climbed the steep slope above the cave, and started for the bluffs that were still higher than their cave sanctuary. At last, out of breath and where he could see the purple light try to slip over the rim of the Mazatzals, he scoped the bluffs for any sign of sheep.

Then a ram came out on a point and looked over the country under his throne. Slocum set the telescope down and picked up his rifle, praying the animal's curiosity lasted a few seconds more. Rifle to his shoulder, he took aim using a large rock outcropping to steady his shot. The rifle's report rippled across the land.

The buck crumpled and fell twenty or so feet off the rim. Then he hit hard in the steep talus, and slid down another fifty or more feet. Satisfied, Slocum reloaded the Winchester and then started across the hillside to get his game.

The ram had a curl in his horns, but he was still young and fat. He'd make good eating. Shouldering his carcass and then picking up his rifle, Slocum headed back for the cave. Ernie once told him he could easily live off this land. Slocum planned to catch some quail next. With a lurch, he squared his heavy load over his shoulder.

"I heard the shot," Amy said, coming up the hill in the purple light to meet him.

"Figured I might get one if I got up there early enough."

"You sure got a big one," she said, looking it over when he paused on the game trail. "Let me have that rifle. I can carry that at least."

They spent the morning skinning and dressing the mountain sheep. His carcass was hung up high under a wet canvas shroud that would keep it cool by evaporation. Then they enjoyed a meal of liver and kidneys. Afterward, she split the skull open, took out the brains to use to tan the hide, and set in to clean off all the meat and fat they'd left on the underside of the skin. That job completed, she stretched the skin tight over a willow frame to dry.

Seated on the old Navajo rug, Slocum spent the rest of the day cleaning their pistols and rifles. Well-oiled guns answered a man's needs. There was no place for a misfire due to poor seating or gummed-up works. When a man lived by guns, lots of care went into keeping them ready. Expecting more trouble was finally the most important factor behind his concern about their firearms.

"Tomorrow we better make the rounds checking cattle," said Amy. "It's Wednesday. Thursday, we work the south end, and Friday, we can work the country around the ramada. Then we can cross that country on Saturday and Sunday and be in Prescott on Monday and hope the governor's there."

"That sounds like good planning to me." Slocum finished oiling down the barrel of the '73 Winchester.

"Do you really think we'll do any damn good up there?"

"Hey, I'm counting on it, sister." He looked down the rifle barrel and, satisfied the bore was clean from all his effort, set the gun aside and sat back on the rock underneath the high ceiling. Someone had to listen to them in Prescott, he figured.

She walked down to the twenty-foot-tall cave entrance and surveyed the vast country beyond with her hands on her hips. A few buzzards floating across the azure sky were in search of an easy meal.

She turned to look back at him. "I think we should spend the rest of the day in a bedroll," she said.

He laughed, and it echoed back in the depth of the underground reaches. "I'm damn sure willing."

She looked back and nodded. "You know you're spoiling me."

"Why, hell, I'd spoil you plumb rotten."

He eased up and strode down to where she stood. Hugging her from behind, he squeezed her to him. "You just need some escape from all the pressures that this has put upon you."

In an instant, she turned around in his grasp and their demanding mouths met. Hungry, wet with lashing tongues, and drawing from each other the power to rise up to a feverish pitch of desire. His hands cupping her firm derriere and her breasts pressed against him.

Ernie, honest to God, we're going to get you out of that hellhole.

4

There were some thin clouds heading south in the predawn light, with a wind shift to the north. The fire Amy cooked over felt good as Slocum rubbed his hands together and absorbed the reflected heat.

"Turned cold last night," she said, and hugged her arms. She was busy frying some sheep meat in a skillet, and a Dutch oven full of biscuits was cooking on the ground beside her.

He rubbed his palms on the front of his pants and yawned. "You doing better?"

She nodded. "I hate winter. This old cave is as close as I have come to a house." She motioned with the long-handled fork at its dark interior. "There isn't much to that ramada down there. No walls, and it gets damn cold in Arizona, especially up here."

"What would you do? I mean, when it got cold."

She grinned big. "We stayed in the bedroll when we were in camp. We never got too tired of doing that or I guess he'd've built a shack."

Slocum shook his head. Those two were a pair. Amy'd been her father's cowboy, and never knew she wasn't a boy or as good as one, until Ernie came along and they got married. Her poor mother cried when she left Texas with her new husband—her daddy turned his back on her and never said good-bye. That hurt her. Slocum had heard the story before.

After breakfast, they loaded the packhorse. She stowed some things in the tin-lined wooden boxes, extra canned goods and other items. It would lighten the packhorse's load, and the supplies would be there when Slocum and Amy returned.

The morning sunlight was trying to cross over the top of the Mazatzal Range when they set out off the mountain for the first day of the "cow check." By her tally, there were 120 mother cows, most with calves trailing them, twenty long yearling heifers Ernie was keeping for cows, six Hereford or Durham bulls, and a hundred or so steers and heifers Ernie planned to sell that fall.

"It was going to be our biggest sale so far," she said, pushing her horse off on a steep game trail. Behind her, the packhorse spooked and then shied back at a juniper in his face.

"Drop the lead," Slocum said, seeing the problem. "He'll come along."

She disappeared around the bend from the horse's sight, and the loaded animal dodged the boughs and hurried to join her.

"Where was I?" she asked over her shoulder with the packhorse recovered.

"Talking about a big sale this fall."

"Yes, well, you can see that's impossible now."

"I bet we can hire some hands in Prescott to help us."

"And get them killed, too. Like they killed that poor fella on the same night as I hired him."

"No," he said, strongly enough that they probably heard him in Oxbow ten miles away. "Old Man Yates and his crew aren't riding roughshod over us as long as I'm here."

"Good. That's what I wanted when I wrote you. Someone as tough as Ernie. That's why they framed him. They were afraid of him."

Slocum nodded, and they spooked up a set of yearlings.

He and Amy trotted to the right, and then turned on the hillside to size them up. Good-looking roan and brockle-faced cross cattle—what the buyers wanted. Ernie knew the cattle breeding business, and his good bulls produced some great offspring. They'd bring a high price when they got to the railhead.

Slocum and Amy rode on, and located Oscar at the next water tank. The oldest bull she owned got up leisurely, and wrung his white-ended tail after arching his back in a stretch.

"Ain't he pretty?" She motioned to the sire. "Cost enough. He should be pretty."

Slocum laughed. "He's paying for himself."

He studied the cautious set of cows and calves standing back and watching them like they were a red wolf passing through. As he watered their horses, he nodded in approval. "Ernie needs to be back for you, and these cattle need him. You two have done well here the past three years."

She agreed, and they rode on.

An hour later in the White Tank Wash, he spotted a late calf with what he considered a fresh brand. He shook out the reata on his saddle and told her he wanted to catch the little guy. He set spurs to Red, the gelding bailed in after the calf, and Slocum made a loop, swinging it over his head. He reached out hoping to snare the calf before he made it into the chaparral. The loop settled over his head, Slocum jerked slack, and then dallied the tail around the horn. Red set down, and the calf was swung around.

Slocum tied the reata to the horn and stepped down. He went down the line and flanked the calf—then stood looking down at the brand and shaking his head. It was a 103 all right.

"How many have they done that to?" she asked, riding up.

"Time will tell. But we need a brand inspector up here that Cummings and Yates don't own."

Stern-faced, she nodded in agreement.

Slocum released the red roan calf, who ran off bawling to his half-longhorn mama. How many more calves had those "innocent" Albert boys branded with a 103? He recoiled up his rope and tied it on the saddle. Amy and the 7C were being attacked from more than one side. Yates and the Albert boys. And who were the masked rapists—some hirelings of Yates? Plenty of unanswered questions.

They rode on hoping to get this section of the range checked out and make the ramada by nightfall.

The cloud cover had thickened by sundown when they made their destination. She dug out a long-tail wool coat for herself, and found a canvas duster to fit him. While she made supper, he put feed bags on the three horses and fed them barley. It wasn't his favorite feed for them, but it was what they grew down in the Salt River Valley and was available. Beards on the seed head sometimes lodged in a horse's throat and caused them to cough and cough until they came free.

He finished up, and came to squat in the reflective heat of her metal stove while she worked on frying potatoes and more sheep meat.

"That mutton ain't half bad," he said when she turned it over in the skillet.

"It sure ain't. Two more days and we head across country, right?"

He nodded. "You worried about that trip?"

"I'm worried the governor'll turn us down. I guess that's why I never went. He's the last one we can talk to and if he says no—" She shook her head and chewed on her lower lip. "That means there is no hope of getting Ernie out."

He rose and squeezed her shoulder to reassure her. "He'll see our point."

"I sure hope so."

After supper, he took their bedroll up on the rise above the shade and spread it on the ground. She trailed behind, acting worn out from the day's ride.

"They're less likely to find us up here," he said.

She agreed, and hugged him. "I'm learning."

Sometime during the night, Slocum awoke at a sound and covered her mouth with his calloused palm. "Hush, we've got company."

Then, down at the ramada, three or four riders began milling around shouting and firing shots. She tried to stop him, but he was up and running with the six-gun in hand. He aimed at a silhouette, his gun belched a flame, and the rider pitched off his horse. Another reined around and clicked his empty pistol at Slocum in the dim light. A bad move. Slocum shot him, and he flew off the butt of his horse.

She was down there by then, wearing only a shirt and using a rifle to shoot at the riders. The others raced off to save themselves.

"How many did you get?" she asked.

"Two. Get a lamp. We'll see if they're alive."

He found the first one he came to lying on his side and moaning. She brought the lamp over and scowled at the man. "Jeff Grant, who works for Yates."

They found the other rider sitting up and holding his left shoulder. "Gawdamn you—"

Slocum kicked him in the face with his bare foot, and sprawled him on his back. Then he put his sole on the wounded man's chest. "You came to kill us. You'll be lucky if I don't hang you."

"What'll we do with them?' she asked.

"Haul them into Oxbow and let the rest of Yates's crew see what happens to raiders. If Cummings won't arrest them, maybe the good people of Oxbow will take the law in their own hands and use some cottonwood justice on them."

"I'll find the horse team—" She looked around in the night as if searching for them.

"Hell, no, they rode in here. They can ride out or go belly down over the saddle. I want folks to see the Yates brand on their horses. He wants war, we'll give him some of his own medicine.

"What's this one's name?" Slocum looked at the raider he'd spilled on his back. The man didn't answer.

Slocum kicked him with his bare foot, and the man grunted, "Saryle Booth."

"All right, Booth, I'm going to collect your horses. You get on your feet. You try something, she'll kill you. You'll probably live if you don't, but if I ever see you again, you better be running the other way, 'cause I'll kill you dead. Savvy?"

"Yeah."

"See you do. I ever see either of you again after today, you're dead meat.'

"You don't own—"

Slocum leaned over and jerked him up to a sitting position with a fistful of his wool vest. His mouth only inches from Booth's, he spat out the words. "I mean dead, you stupid sumbitch. You *comprehende*?"

He released Booth. "Who were the others?"

No answer.

"Go get me a sharp knife," he said to her. "He don't need his ears, he don't use 'em."

"All right. Tom Smith and Bob Jones."

"They real people?" Slocum asked Amy.

"I don't think so."

Slocum grabbed Booth's right ear and twisted it hard. "I'll skin it off your head if you don't go to telling me the truth."

Booth tried to make him stop, but his efforts obviously hurt his wounded shoulder and he quit. "All right, Nick Tarrel and Snuffy Carlson."

"They work for Yates," she said.

"Everyone works for Yates," Slocum said, conscious that he was naked save for the pistol in his hand and the night wind was cold on his bare skin. "I'll go get dressed."

"Why now? We've all seen it." She laughed anxiously.

He shook his head on the way back to the bedroll. This job didn't get any easier.

A colder gust off the Mongollon Rim swept in and liked to froze him. He had goose bumps all over his body when he finally got dressed. Shivering, he strapped on his gun belt, and then he swept up the bedroll and duster. Looked like sleeping was over for the night anyway.

The four rode into Oxbow in mid-morning. Soon, Slocum saw the town's population began to ooze outside to see the two bareheaded prisoners with their hands tied to their saddle horns, and from the blood, new and old, on their shirts, it was obvious they had been wounded. Both Slocum and Amy carried rifles over their laps. Some men came out of the Irish Saloon. Slocum addressed them.

"These two, along with Nick Tarrel and Snuffy Carlson, raided Mrs. Branch's place last night. They were shooting to kill, except we had changed our bedrooms and moved uphill. The law won't stop this, then I think it's time that the citizens of this town get a rope ready for this kind.

"We caught two rustlers this week and took them to Globe. They were the Albert brothers, Nathan and Webb. The sheriff refused to do anything about them—" He turned to Amy.

"Cummings called them innocent boys," she said to the crowd, and by this time there were several people listening. "We found another of my calves they'd put a one-oh-three brand on yesterday."

"Who owns that brand?" an older man asked. "I've got two of them they did that to."

"Some cattle buyer named Drithers. He's going to pay them half the claim money that they send him for them."

"What can we do?" one man asked.

"Shoot any one of these four men mentioned here on sight. We can clean up this end of Gila County."

One stern-looking woman stepped off the boardwalk. "Those men need medical attention. Aren't you going to do anything?"

Slocum pushed in close and cut loose Booth's hands from the horn. Then he shoved him off out of the saddle, and Booth fell to the ground with a scream. He simply lay there.

"Why, I never—" the woman protested.

"Listen, they rode into Mrs. Branch's place last night shooting real bullets at where they thought we were sleeping. Ma'am, they'd've not even sent flowers to our funerals if we died." He spurred Red in close and did cut Grant loose the same way. "Now, you can fix them up or let them die. I don't care. Send word to Yates. Let him tend them. They're his hired hands."

"What's your name, mister?"

"Slocum." He looked over the hard-eyed crowd of women, children, and men. "Tell Yates I said he better not try anything else, or I'll bring his carcass in here for the buzzards to pick his eyes out."

He nodded at Amy and they rode out.

"Yates know about this?" she asked under her breath as she looked back at the settlement from the road headed south.

"Sure, those other two didn't let their shirttails hit their asses until they rode back and told him his plan had blown up."

She nodded. "I never saw you that mad before as you were in Oxbow."

"I haven't been that mad in a while, but this business has me upset."

"It's going to rain," she said, and looked up at the buttermilk sky.

"It never rains in Arizona," he teased.

"Oh, sometimes it rains too much." Then she laughed.

Amy being amused sounded good to him, even if it was part of the tension they shared on the knife edge they straddled, without any law and with Yates trying to push her out.

They had lots of work to do.

5

Saturday morning, they started for Prescott. Packhorse in tow, they camped on the Verde River that evening, and the next day rode up through Bloody Basin, and reached Mayer the second night. He bought her a meal in a café, and then they rode on quite a ways farther, camping in Prescott Valley. Before dawn, they were up and rode on into the state capital.

Bob Park's Livery was where Slocum stabled his horses there. He knew Bob from the days when Slocum had hauled the mail from Gallup, New Mexico, to Prescott. Road weary, he dropped out of the saddle heavily at the open double doors, and nodded to her as Amy did the same.

A swamper came out with a receipt pad, licking a lead pencil. "What's the name and how long you leaving 'em?"

"Till I get ready to leave. Parks around?"

"No, he's gone to see about buying some hay. I'm Oswald."

"Grain 'em and wipe them down."

"That'll be an extra two bits."

"I can afford it." He removed his saddlebags and she took the carpetbag that contained her dress off her saddle, and

42

they left the ponies with Oswald. Slocum carried everything, and they walked down the steep hill toward the courthouse.

"Reckon the governor's even here?" she asked.

"His office is up on that hill beyond Whiskey Row." He pointed to the row of saloons facing the new courthouse.

"You know him?"

Slocum shook his head. "But he's just a man, and he probably can make some sense of this entire deal."

"I hope so. Lord, I hope so. Where we going first?"

"Sudsie Hale has a café down here. And she makes some great pecan pie."

"Then we go see Governor Sterling?"

"We'll probably need to make an appointment first."

"What's that mean?"

"Get a time in his appointment book to speak to him about your problems."

She raised her eyebrows and looked to the sky for help. "I get awful anxious thinking I'm going to be speaking for poor Ernie." She looked hard after some riders who went past them. "Did you hear that man's voice rode by us just now?"

"Which one?"

"The one in the gray hat. The big man riding with those three."

Slocum looked at their backs. The large man and the three younger men, almost kids, were riding some jaded horses downhill toward Whiskey Row. "Who are they?"

"That man sounded just like the one that raped me."

"You recognize his voice?"

"Yes, I'm sure it's him. Big, kinda rusty-sounding. What are we going to do?"

"I want you to go to Sudsie's Café and wait for me. He may remember you if he gets a better look at you. He don't know me."

"There's four of them," she said, looking upset.

"So? Those three boys ain't no threat. He'd be the one to worry about."

She nodded. "What are you going to do?"

"Drink a beer or two and learn who they are first. You go to the right on the next corner, and her place is in the basement half a block down. Stay there. I'll be coming. Tell her I sent you."

"Slocum, be careful."

"I will, and then we can go make an appointment to see the governor."

After they parted, Slocum spotted the four men's horses hitched out front of the Palace Saloon, and he sauntered inside. He saw "Gray Hat" sitting at a table with his three associates, and they all were giving the bar girl a hard time. She finally nodded, looking disgusted at the four, and returned to the bar.

"I could kill that Chelsey Farnam at times," she said through her teeth to the bartender.

The dark-featured man laughed. "He needs it. What's his order?"

"Four beers. One with an egg in it." She looked back at them again, then in disgust she stared at the back-bar mirror with a scowl. "Sumbitch offered me fifty cents to service all four of them. Cheap bastard."

Slocum, nursing a mug of beer, slid fifty cents down the bar toward her.

She curled her lip and looked suspiciously at the money. "What do you need?"

"Some information. Who's with him?"

"The same bunch as always. Tad Boyd, Boles Carter, and Fargo Tompkins."

He nodded, looking at the large mule deer rack over the back-bar mirror. "What do they do for a living?"

"They probably fuck sheep. I don't know." She thanked the bartender when he brought the four mugs of beer. She looked hard at the glass that had the egg in it. Satisfied, she took the tray and went to serve their drinks.

Slocum watched her in the mirror. He could see her deliver them, and Farnam pinched her ass in the process. She slapped his hand aside and told him it would be sixty cents.

"Sixty cents?"

"Sam, tell him the price." She tossed her head at the bartender.

Sam slung a towel over his shoulder, stepped up to the bar, and nodded. "You owe the lady sixty cents."

"Lady?" Farnam laughed out loud. "She's just some little cunt."

"Farnam, either pay her or get the hell out of here." Sam laid a sawed-off shotgun on the bar. "Take your drinking somewhere else."

"I'm paying her, gawdamnit." Farnam rose and dug in his pants pocket for the money.

"One more outburst out of you, and I'll come over this bar and you'll regret it," said Sam.

"You talk big with a damn shotgun."

"You through mouthing off?" Sam demanded, looking hard enough at him to drive nails.

The situation soon settled down. The barmaid came over and bumped against Slocum with her small butt. "You needing company? I get off at five."

"No. I just need some information on those four men."

"What for? They're losers."

"I think they were the bunch raped my best friend's wife over in Gila County."

With her right hand, she swept back the hair from her face, then lowered her voice. "They answer her description?"

"To a T."

"You going to have them arrested?"

"The Gila County sheriff won't get off his ass and do anything."

"So?"

"So, I may set their tails on fire."

"Can I help you? That damn Farnam raped me once, too, when I first came to work here."

Slocum lifted his mug and studied the ring of water left on the bar surface, Then he looked over the rim of his beer at the small woman, hardly more than a girl, in a low-cut blouse and skirt. "I don't doubt it." He lowered his voice. "Where does he live?"

"Somewhere down the Black Canyon Road."

He slid her two more quarters down the bar under his fingertips. "Don't tell them a thing."

"Oh, mister," she said under her breath, "I won't tell them anything." She flounced off to wait on two men who came in and took a table.

Good. "Sam, bring me another beer."

Sam brought it over and set it down, looking hard at Slocum. "Weren't you the fella delivered the Christmas mail a few years back when they were having all those robberies?"

"Keep it a secret."

"I will, but that was neat." Sam made a swipe at the bar surface with his rag. "Sorry I had to get that scattergun out. Farnam pisses me off at times."

"More than you," Slocum said, looking in the mirror at the four.

After he finished his beer, he hiked over to Sudsie's and at a side table, Amy looked up from her coffee with a wide grin. "How did it go?"

"I have their names and where they live anyway."

"Good. Who are they?"

"His name is—" The sound of the buxom Sudsie's voice shut his words off as she rushed out of the kitchen.

"Slocum, where in the hell have you been, you old rascal?" She hurried over and threw out her arms to hug him.

Standing astraddle the chair, he held her ripe form to his body. She finally stood back and looked him over like she was examing a horse she planned to buy. "You know he saved the day around here at Christmas a few years ago?"

Amy nodded. "He told me some about it."

"Some? Why, there was mail scattered from here to Gallup, and he straightened it up and got the fellas robbing it as well. Sit down. She said she needed to see the governor."

"Yes, the law back where she comes from framed her husband and refused to prosecute two cattle rustlers because they were so-called innocent boys."

Sudsie shook her head and then sat across from them. Tucking tufts of her wavy graying hair back in under pins, she shook her head. "Damn crooks are bad enough. But using the law for their operations is worse."

"Chelsey Farnam?" Slocum asked.

"A damn bully."

"What else do you know about him?"

"Folks use him to collect money for them." Sudsie shook her head. "Amy told me about him, too, if it's the one you trailed down to the row. I figured it was Farnam. Lives inches from the law."

"But rape?" asked Slocum.

"Hard to prove, ain't it?" Sudsie shook her head in disgust.

Slocum nodded. "The barmaid at the Palace said he raped her, too."

"Who's a jury going to believe if there are no witnesses?" Sudsie clutched her hands together on the tabletop and shared a nod with Amy.

"I guess you're right," Slocum said, still trying to figure out how to bring him to justice. "Now about Governor Sterling. I don't know him."

"Typical appointee that President Grant sends out here. He damn sure ain't no cowboy." Then Sudsie laughed aloud. "But I think he's fair. Hey, I'll feed you folks and we can talk more later."

They agreed, and she hurried off to the kitchen.

"Learn anything else about them?" Amy asked in a soft voice.

"They're obviously enforcers that hire out."

She made a peeved face at him. "I guess there isn't anything we can do about them?"

"I'm working on that right now." Then he reached over to squeeze her hand. "I promise you we'll get him and his bunch."

They ate sliced roast beef, fresh green beans, boiled potatoes and gravy, with Sudsie's fresh-sliced sourdough bread, and washed down with good coffee. Amy used the back room to change into a dress.

Slocum thanked Sudsie when she refused to take any money, and he and Amy headed for the log capitol building on the hill in the direction of Thumb Butte, the distinct rock chimneylike formation made aeons before when the earth took shape.

"I sure feel undressed wearing a dress," Amy said.

"You look nice in one."

"You and Ernie Branch. *You look good in a dress*. I feel like . . . well . . . I can't say it."

Slocum laughed.

"It isn't funny. I wonder what the governor'll tell us."

"Be calm. He's just another man."

"Wish I had your coolness right now."

Several people sat in the lobby when they arrived. Slocum and Amy walked up to the desk and spoke to the person in charge, a man with gold wire-rimmed glasses who acted very nervous and fidgety.

"I can't guarantee—I mean he may run out of time to talk to you today—see Governor Sterling—well, he has—have a seat—if he has time, I'll call you, Miss—"

"*Mrs*. Amy Branch of Oxbow," she corrected him.

"Yes, yes. Mrs. I am sorry. You two have a seat."

Time clicked slowly by on the schoolhouse clock, but by five ten they were shown into the governor's office. A tall thin man in his forties rose, shook their hands, and told them to take a chair in front of his large walnut desk.

When he asked them the nature of their business, Amy explained about her husband being framed. The well-dressed governor nodded as she spoke, leaning back in his wing-backed wooden chair and making the springs creak. He listened intently to her every word, put his index finger to his mouth at times, and a serious concern shone in his brown eyes.

"Then, besides that—" Amy quit and looked over at Slocum.

"A gang of thugs from over here in Prescott raped her before I got there to help her," Slocum said, coming to her rescue. "And the law would do nothing about it. They wore masks, and since she had no names at that time, they did nothing."

Sterling held up his hand. "I want U.S. Marshal Sam Hendren to hear about this. I'll be just a moment. I'll call him in here."

When the governor strode out of the room, she quickly frowned at Slocum as if to get his reaction.

"He's listening anyway," Slocum said to reassure her.

She bobbed her head, swallowed hard, and looked half sick with worry.

Sam Hendren was five-eight, much shorter than his boss, and wore a bushy salt and pepper mustache curled in the corners like cattle horns. His hair was thin on top. He shook hands with both of them.

Sterling in guarded words brought him up to date on Ernie's conviction and her multiple rape. Hendren nodded when Sterling finished, and then he looked at them. "Who were those men, ma'am?"

She deferred to Slocum.

"Chelsey Farnam. Along with Tad Boyd, Boles Carter, and Fargo Tompkins. That's all that I know about them."

Hendren made a sour face and shook his head. "They're damn sure troublemakers and in on many shady deals. I'm sorry, ma'am."

She nodded.

Slocum then continued her story for her. "A week ago, we caught two men old enough to know better branding one of her calves, and we took them to Globe to Sheriff Cummings, and he would not lock them up. Said they were just innocent boys."

Tenting his fingers under the tip of his nose and leaning back in his chair, Sterling scowled. "How old were they?"

"Eighteen to twenty. Not kids," Slocum said.

"What do you think, Sam?"

Hendren, who sat beside them, put his arm on the desk. "Where should I start?"

"Maybe at Yuma Territorial Prison. I want a report on my desk about her husband's case next week if we can get it. Now, Mrs. Branch, don't get your hopes up too high. This all could take months. I can't simply pardon a man until I have the entire case investigated. I know that other governors operated differently. But I will consider his case, and Sam will also look into the law enforcement part."

"Thank you," she said demurely.

"Now, where can I find you, ma'am?" Marshal Hendren asked.

"Her 7C Ranch is south of Oxbow," Slocum said. "But she doesn't stay at her headquarters since the incident. You show up, we'll find you."

"I can understand why. Thanks, I'll be showing up there quick as I can." Hendren dropped his face and shook his head. "That Chelsey Farnam is one of those fellas that walks the narrow path, but he'll fall."

"It sounds like the territory would be much better off without him," Sterling said. "And, Mrs. Branch, I am truly sorry about you husband's situation and I will investigate his case as quickly as I can."

"Thank you," she said.

They all shook hands, and Slocum led her out the door.

"What do you think?" she whispered, leaving the building.

"He listened to it all."

She nodded, and then he saw a trembling in her shoulders under her dress.

"Quit worrying. It's going to work."

"It's got to. Ernie's still in jail."

Somehow, they'd figure a way to get him released. All the lawmen in the territory weren't being paid off. Somehow . . .

6

He blew out the lamp on the nightstand, and their hotel room was engulfed in darkness. Toeing off his boots, he could see her shedding the dress in the pearly light coming in the room's window. Soon, she shrugged the sleeves off, and the sway of her pear-shaped breasts made his heartbeat quicken. Stepping out of the dress, she carefully put it over the chair.

"I'm sure glad to be out of that getup."

He shed his pants and hung them on the wall peg, then his vest and shirt. "You mean you don't want to be a lady?"

"No, sirree."

"Well," he said, taking her hands in his and admiring her in the dim light. "You'd have to really work to hide it."

She raised her chin and smiled up at him. "Glad you like it."

They soon began kissing, pressing raw flesh to raw flesh. Her skin felt cool against his. Their hungry mouths were feeding on the passion in both of them. Tongues lashing and her firm breasts gouging him, his erection a shaft between them.

Her fingers soon clutched his cock possessively and she pulled on it gently at first, but as their flames grew brighter, it felt like an iron fist was holding him. At last, out of breath, she tore her mouth from his and said, "I want you now."

He swept her up in his arms and set her gently on the bed, then crawled in on top of her. Then he raised up and listened.

"That's their room—," someone said in the hall.

"Get in the corner quick," Slocum whispered, and rolled off her, hitting the floor and filling his fist with the Colt in the holster on the ladder-back chair.

A boot at the knob smashed the door open, and two six-guns sprayed the room, filling it with gun smoke and ear-shattering reports. Crouched to the side, Slocum fired his .44 pistol, and took out the two gunmen, who crumpled in the fog of gunfire and onto the floor in the darkened hall. The thundering sound of a man's fleeing boots going for the back door echoed in the hall.

"You all right?" Slocum asked Amy.

"Yes—" She coughed on the fog of stinking gun smoke in the air.

"Better get dressed. We'll have lots of company up here in a short while." He pulled on his pants and then his shirt. Seated on the bed, he put on socks and boots. Already there were folks calling out. "Is any one alive up here?"

"Yes. We'll be out in a minute." He looked at her in the dark room, and saw she was practically dressed.

He opened the window for more air, and then went to the doorway. Someone had relit the hall lamp. Both men on the floor looked dead. He picked up their handguns, tossing them aside.

Then he looked up at the flush-faced young desk clerk. "Who was the third fella?"

"What?" The word stuck in his throat. He shook his head numbly, which told Slocum almost enough.

"The other fella who came in here with these two."

The clerk swallowed hard. "I didn't get a good look at him—sir."

"What in the hell's name's all the shooting about?" a voice sounding like someone in authority shouted from the stairs. Soon, a man wearing a badge showed up with his hat on the back of his head.

"Three men came to kill us," Slocum said

"Excuse my French, ma'am," the lawman said to Amy. "Who're these two?"

"Tompkins and Carter were the names given to me earlier."

"What happened?" The scowl on the town marshal's craggy face looked serious.

"They broke in the door and came in shooting. I returned fire."

"Were there more than this?"

"Yes. One ran out that back door. Unscathed, I guess."

"Holy Christmas. You reckon they're both dead?" He indicated the pair on the floor.

"They sure ain't kicking," Slocum said, shoving the Colt in his waistband.

"I can see that. My name's Moriarity."

"Slocum is mine. This is Mrs. Branch."

He swept off his hat and shook her hand. "Sorry, ma'am. Our town is usually much quieter than this."

She nodded, obviously still shaken by the turn of events.

"What are you going to do with the bodies?" Slocum asked.

"I guess bury them after the coroner examines them. They've sent for him. I left my man Fred downstairs to stem the tide of curious who no doubt are just busting to view them. Ralph." Moriarity turned to the clerk. "Go find these two another room. This door frame is busted, and besides, the damn gun smoke is bad in here."

Moriarity turned on his heel at the approach of someone coming up the stairs. "Howdy, Doc. Got you some coroner business. They look past patching up."

The man behind the gold-rimmed glasses nodded, set down his case, and drew out a stethoscope to listen to the first one's heart. He nodded. "He's dead."

"I think they both are," Moriarity said.

Doc then listened to the second one's heart and agreed. He climbed to his feet and wound up the cords of his stethoscope. "Send them over to Tully's funeral home. I'll do an autopsy on them over there."

"Be a hearing at the courthouse nine in the morning," Moriarity said. "Doc, you and Slocum and Mrs. Branch will be there."

The clerk returned and handed Slocum another key.

"Who was with these two?" the lawman asked the clerk, who was staying clear of the dead like they were sidewinders.

"Another man, I guess."

"You know, because they came right to this room," Slocum said. "So you told them where we were staying."

"All right. All right. But he said he'd kill me if I told a soul. It was Chelsey Farnam."

The lawman looked at Slocum. "Well, now we know the man," said Moriarity. "Why would he want to kill you?"

"Probably wanted her dead," Slocum said. "Him and another man plus these two all raped her, and he might be afraid she was filing a warrant for their arrest."

"Was she?"

Slocum shook his head. "But she recognized his voice yesterday from the crime and he knew it."

"I'm sorry, ma'am. But do you recognize these two?"

Amy stepped forward. "I believe that one has a bad scar on his butt. I'd say a bull once gored him. And the other one has knife scars on his belly. They wore masks."

Doc knelt down and unbuttoned the man's bloody shirt. "This one has knife scars."

She nodded. "That other one has the scars from the goring he got."

"You mentioned another one besides Farnam?" Moriarity asked.

"That one never touched me," she said. "I don't know anything about him. I can't even place his voice."

Some men arrived with two stretchers, and soon the bodies and Doc were gone. Slocum and Amy got ready to move to the room down the hall.

"The coroner's hearing will be at nine at the courthouse," said Moriarity.

"We'll be there," Slocum said after him.

When Slocum and Amy were in a fresh room, she collapsed in his arms. "My God, I could hardly believe what you did. I was so lost."

"It'll be fine. Farnam will answer for tonight, and we might get him for rape as well." He rocked her back and forth in his arms. "It's going to be okay. I think when Sterling learns about Yates's conspiracy, Ernie will be pardoned."

"God, I hope so."

"We better get some sleep. Nine will come early."

After breakfast at Sudsie's, they walked the block and a half to the Yavapai County Courthouse. Inside the building, they followed the directions of a young man to the courtroom.

Moriarity and a young man in a suit met them there. The man in the suit was from the prosecutor's office; his name Ned Whorton. He asked Slocum some questions, then looked satisfied.

"Obviously, Mr. Slocum, this was a matter of self-defense. I am sure Justice Stanley will see it that way."

"I would hope so."

The hearing proceeded with a report from the coroner. Doc took off his gold-rimmed glasses after he told them about the wounds sustained by the two men, and looked at the judge. "I'd say those two over there was damned lucky to be alive."

"Doc, I agree. Now, there was an accomplice who escaped, Mr. Whorton?"

Whorton called the desk clerk to the stand and under oath, he admitted that Chelsey Farnam had demanded to know Slocum's room number, and then all three men had rushed upstairs, Farnam, Tompkins, and Carter. They had their guns drawn.

"Their guns drawn?" the magistrate asked.

The clerk swallowed hard. "Their guns drawn and cocked, sir."

"They say why they wanted Mr. Slocum and Mrs. Branch?"

"They did lots of cussing."

"What did they cuss about?"

"Those two, I guess."

"Very good. You are dismissed.

"Mr. Slocum, please rise. I don't need you under oath. But I would like you to tell me any notion you may have on why they'd want to kill you or Mrs. Branch?"

"May I approach the bench, Your Honor?"

"'Yes. Come over."

"Your Honor, those men raped Mrs. Branch about a month ago. Gila County officials refused to investigate the crime. These men knew that we knew who they were, and wanted to stop us from testifying."

The judge bobbed his head. "Sorry we had to take this long to find you not guilty, but now it shall be on the record—self-defense. Not guilty, and swear out a murder warrant for this Chelsey Farnam."

"Murder, sir?" his recorder asked.

"Yes, murder—he got those two boys with him killed for starters."

Judge Stanley slammed the gavel down and declared the proceedings ended. He signaled to Slocum to come over to the side of the bench. His hand extended, he pumped Slocum's. "I thought I recognized you. You're the fella that got the mail line back running a few years ago. Mighty fine shooting. Glad you or her weren't hurt. You planning to stay around Prescott?"

"No, sir. She has a ranch over in Gila County, and we'll need to get back over there and run it."

"You ever need my help, just holler. Ma'am, you'll have good help."

"What are the chances of the sheriff here getting Chelsey Farnam?"

"Oh, good. They've been trying to hang something on that no-account for several years. Now we have a crime to charge him with. Unless he runs out of our jurisdiction, he'll be behind bars in a matter of days."

Slocum and Amy left the courthouse and went by to tell

Sudsie good-bye. She dried her hands on a towel and hugged Amy, then him. "You two be careful going home. Farnam isn't in jail yet and he's sure a back-shooter."

"We'll be careful and thanks," Slocum said.

"Did you and her have an affair once?" Amy asked when they were outside and headed for the livery.

"I reckon so. Once we did."

She laughed. "Well, I'm sure glad it's my turn is all I am going to say."

He looked over and saw her face was beet red. He shook her shoulder and laughed some himself.

When their horses were saddled, they rode out for the ranch, leading the loaded packhorse. She'd added some staples to their panniers. They reached the Verde by evening and made camp. He gathered firewood and she started the fire. Cottonwood was not the greatest fuel, but they made do with it along with some dead sycamore.

She fried some bacon and new potatoes, and boiled some fresh green beans. Then, while a coyote yodeled at the rising quarter moon, they sat cross-legged on the ground and ate her delicious food, washing it down with good hot coffee.

"You amaze me, Amy."

"How's that?" Her face was highlighted in the glow of the fire.

"Most women wouldn't live in a ramada for a home. Let alone ride this cactus-infested range."

"Hey, this ranch is my dream, too, brother. Ernie never asked me about my past. I never asked him about his. He told me before we got married that he thought in ten years we'd have a real ranch, if we tried hard. I believed it would have worked, too, except for that greedy Yates, who came along wanting to hog up everything."

"You two will have that ranch. I believe that, too."

"You really think we did some good back there at Prescott?"

"Oh, we have. Farnam's on the run anyway. They may even be able to tie him to Yates. We get that done, your main obstacle will be eliminated. Sterling pardons Ernie and you two are back building a ranch."

"Sounds easy as hell."

He blew the steam off his tin coffee cup.

"What are you thinking?" she asked.

"I'm thinking we'll be back on the ranch in two days. I'd like to take the fight to Yates."

"But how?"

"I'm not certain, but I think we can start doing small things to them. Get the simple hands spooked."

"Will it work?"

"We go to spooking his help and get them to quit the country, it will work on the old man too."

"I'm game to anything that will stop him."

He winked at her. "We'll start when we get back."

"More coffee?"

He nodded, and she bounded to her feet, slapping off the seat of her pants on the way to the fire. "I hope we're doing as good as we can by Ernie."

"Nothing short of an angel extracting him would be any better."

She shook her head hard as she brought the pot back. "Ain't any angel coming for Ernie."

They both laughed.

Hell, he had one waiting for him.

7

Things were going strong in Oxbow on Saturday night. The Irish Saloon was doing a land-office business and horses were hitched at every rack, wagon tongue, and porch post. They must have totaled five dozen. Slocum was looking for Yates horses. They bore a Bar 0 brand, and when he found one, he cut the cinch down to a few strings. While he parted the girths, Amy was looking for the next Yates horse. They moved silently through the masses, and they worked over a dozen horses.

Then they rode up the road, and planted their scarecrow dressed in a white sheet with a horse skull on it and an old cowboy hat. Painted on the front of the sheet was BAR 0 COWBOYS BEWARE in charcoal.

"I wish we could be here when they ride by and see this," said Amy.

"We still have lots more to do," Slocum told her.

She agreed, and they rode off. By daybreak, they had planted POISON signs at three of Yates's tanks and wiped out their own tracks. Then, by making a wide swing, they ended up at the cave by midday. Done in and exhausted, they grained their horses, fell on top of the bedroll, and were soon fast asleep.

When he awoke in late afternoon, she was sitting up brushing her hair. "I am wondering what we should do next," she said.

"Run a spook through their cow camp."

"How do we do that?"

"We make a dummy and sneak off one of their horses to use. Plus the more cowboys we can separate from their horses and force them to walk in, the better it will get."

"Will they get the message?"

"Quicker than you think."

"I've made some coffee."

"Sounds good. We can lay off them for a day or so. That will make them jumpier waiting for something else to happen."

"I've always wondered how he could afford so many hands on his payroll. I couldn't afford that many."

"Some are gunhands, but most of them have to be used to working cattle and doing ranch chores. Someone's coming," he said, and grabbed for his gun.

"It's only Rufus the prospector," she said, getting up. "I can tell by the sound of his burro's hooves."

She waved the old man up to where they were on the ledge. "What's new?" she asked.

Rufus dismounted and smiled. "Why, someone went and cut cinches on the Yates boys' ponies last night." His laughter echoed in the cave. "They were mad as wet hens. It was daylight before they could get the store opened and repair their rigs. Then someone left them a horse-skull scarecrow north of town saying, 'You Yates hands better clear the country.'"

"Reckon any of them did?" she asked.

"Sure. It spooked three of 'em, I think. They were leaving the country according to Pete Ogle, who talked to them.

"I reckon someone besides you two is into it with Yates. No wonder. He's trying to force everyone to leave or else, and the law in Globe won't do a thing to stop him." Rufus made a scowl and shook his bearded face. "I'm glad someone's trying to tree him now. They may get it done, by golly."

"He'll be a tough one to shake."

Rufus agreed with Slocum, and Amy poured the old man some coffee. "Have any of the small ranchers left the country so far?" she asked.

"Yeah. Henrys pulled out maybe a week ago. I come by their place a few days ago and they were gone. All their personal things, too. Drove their cattle out, too. She'd been sickly and had never lived this hard a life back in Tennessee."

"That's a shame," she said. "They made good neighbors. Any more?"

"No, the rest are too poor or bad off to leave." Rufus laughed and slapped his knee, which created a small dust storm.

"The rest have their lives invested in their places," she said.

"Yes, but they may also die there. Ole Man Yates has no hesitation about killing people."

"I wish Ernie was here. He could have brought them together and all of us would have stood up against Yates and the bad law. Slocum and I shot up two of his men for trying to kill us, and some old woman was worried we were mistreating them."

"I heard about that." Rufus looked hard at her. "You're right about Ernie organizing folks against him. Yates knew that, too, and rather than back-shoot him, he had him arrested."

Slocum agreed to himself. Sending Ernie to prison was not just to get him out of the country. It removed him from becoming a leader, and was much better than shooting him in the back and possibly having lots of questions to answer even if Yates owned the law. Yates was no fool, and would be a formidable stinging scorpion until his stinger was extracted.

"Someone poisoned his best spring, too," Rufus said, and chuckled.

"Poisoned it?" she asked.

"Word I got, he had boys up there fencing it off this week until they were certain the poison's all out of it."

"What kinda poison?" Slocum asked.

"Strychnine, I reckon."

"Any animals die from drinking it?" she asked, sounding cautious.

"Naw, they caught them in time, I guess."

"Good," she said. "That's serious business, poisoning a water supply."

"It is. It is. There's someone out to get Yates instead of him getting them."

Sounded exactly the way Slocum wanted it to. Stopping Yates's attacks, running off his help—Yates would soon get the message that he wasn't the only bully in the country.

"I'll fix some supper," Amy said. "You'll stay, won't you?"

"Yes, ma'am. A man would be plumb foolish to run off and not eat your vittles, girl."

Slocum agreed with Rufus, and excused himself to check on their horses. He took some ground barley from the pannier and put it in each feed bag. As soon as the sun went down, the temperature would drop as the calendar moved into fall. The desert wasn't like Montana. But it got cold enough to even touch on frost before sunup on many winter mornings, especially as high as they were. Catclaw, mesquite, paloverde, cholla, and even the towering saguaros made this the land that Mexicans called Chaparral. Bull-hide chaps were a necessity to ward off the millions of thorns ready to poke any man or beast that dared enter the country.

The three horses chewed on the their grain with the feed bags hung on their heads. Since Slocum and Amy hadn't gathered any others to ride, they needed to keep these three in good condition.

It was during the evening meal she'd prepared for them that Rufus edged his way into a conversation. "I ain't telling you . . ."

"What's that?" she asked him as the three sat cross-legged on the cave floor in the dimming twilight.

"Well, Luke at the ferry, you know him, told me a few days ago, if you two ever went back to Globe, to go around the front of the Superstitions."

"Why did he do that? That would be a day farther or more."

"Now, he wasn't dead certain, but he thinks Yates has two of his men watching the road to Globe somewheres between the ferry and the courthouse. He said he likes you and Slocum, and didn't want either of you hurt if he could help it."

She shot a questioning glance at Slocum.

"Thank Luke for us. He's probably right," Slocum said, realizing that the real reason Rufus had come by was to warn them.

The next morning the old man and his burros were gone. Didn't wait for breakfast. Amy acted upset. "He almost never leaves before breakfast."

"He was just respecting our privacy. He's a very private man himself. He's very careful about getting in our way."

She looked up while bent over her cooking. "I guess you're right. What should we do today?"

"Check your cattle and operations. I am amused that Yates is fencing those water tanks because of our signs."

"I was, too. When do you think we'll hear from Sterling?"

"Whenever Sam Hendren shows up."

"How will he find us?"

"I suspect that ole law dog can find us if he wants us. We can check the main ramada and look for a message. It's too short a time for him to get hooked up, I figure, and investigate it all or get a grand jury called up."

She washed her hands and dried them on a flour sack towel. "I about have it ready to eat."

"Good." He stood at a high place from which he could see out the mouth of the cave. The great shadow cast by the mountain range covered the gray brush that cloaked the broken country to the west. He studied the vastness for any sign of a rider or movement. Nothing. Satisfied, he turned and went to join her.

"You concerned about something today?" she asked, handing him the hash-fried potatoes and crisp bacon. He bent over, quickly took two biscuits out of the open Dutch oven, and put them on his tin plate before they could burn his fingertips.

"I'm concerned every hour of the day and night. Yates is a very calculating enemy. Rufus warned us he has the Globe road guarded. If he wasn't afraid of us going there, he wouldn't have guards on the road."

Later, saddled up, they swung north to check water holes and cattle. It was mid-morning when he spotted the first rider.

"You see him?" he asked her, pointing out where the man had disappeared in the catclaw.

She swiveled around. "Who was he?"

"I don't know Yates's men, but that one back there sure didn't want to talk to us." His hand on his gun butt, he surveyed the brushy cover. An army could hide thirty feet behind the row of rider-tall desert shrubs that lined the dry wash.

"In a second or two, we're going racing down this draw, and we'll cut left in the first wide draw, rein up, and take a stand."

She made a quick nod. They put steel spurs to their horses. Slocum expected any moment for a shot to cut the cool air. Both horses tore out in an explosion and they swept around a bend.

A rider with a six-gun in his hand was trying to spur his horse off a three-foot bank and into the wash from their right. The horse was having a head-slinging fit. Then it half reared. Slocum fired two quick offhanded shots at the rider.

The cowboy flew off his mount on the far side. His horse left the country bucking high as the moon and kicking over its back as it headed down the wash. Slocum pointed to a side canyon while looking hard in every direction for more trouble. Around the bend, she drew out the .44/40 repeater from under her right stirrup, and he turned an ear to listen above their hard-breathing horses for any sounds of pursuit.

Impatient and pent up, Red stomped around in a tight circle underneath him, and Slocum checked him.

"Any sound of them?" she asked.

He shook his head.

"That wasn't the same one, was it?"

"No, the other one rode a gray."

"Number two will be lucky to ever get his saddle back. What do we do now?"

Slocum didn't give a damn if the man ever got his gear back or not. He had greater concerns. "I don't think I hit him. But now we can't go back to the cave. They'll for sure backtrack us up there."

"What if we cut them off?"

"Could be dangerous."

"You shielding me?"

He gave her a wry look—of course he was. "You've got to mind me if we try it."

She half laughed at him. "Like I haven't been doing that for days."

He agreed with a nod, swung Red around, and drove him up onto a high point. All he could hear was the *whit-whew* of the Gambel's quail and some doves cooing. Nothing moved. Maybe the old man had only sent two men out to ambush them.

Then, he heard a horse coming loping down the wash, and checked the rifle he still held. He made a sign for her to be still. Two men came in sight riding double. They never looked up until he shouted at them. "Hold it right there and put your hands up."

Looking shocked, they obeyed him, and he gave her a head toss to go cover them. She turned her horse off, and soon held her Colt on them while he came off the hill.

"Who are you?" the black-bearded one asked.

Slocum dismounted. Coming around Red, he shoved the rifle in the scabbard. Then, filled with anger, he jerked the whiskered one out of the saddle and slung him on the ground. "What in the hell is your name?"

Rubbing the sand off his face, the man propped himself up. "Blackie Tarp."

Slocum gave him a quick kick in the ribs. "What the hell are you doing up here?"

The man winced and grabbed his side. "Looking for strays."

"No, you were up here looking to bushwhack us." Slocum

kicked the man's six-gun, which had fallen out of his holster, skittering across the sand. Blackie Tarp had obviously not hit either one of them.

"No, mister—"

The other cowboy, no doubt fearing he'd be the next one on the ground, slid off the horse's butt and held his hands high for Amy to disarm him.

"What's *your* name?" Slocum demanded.

"Goose Napier."

"One of you better start talking or I'm pounding sand down your throats."

"We—we're looking for strays for the outfit—"

Slocum reached down, grasped a handful of Tarp's vest, and jerked him to his feet. "Now tell me your orders or I'm fixing to slap the crap out of you."

"He-he said—"

"Who said?"

"Old Man Yates said he'd pay us a hundred each to get rid of you."

Filled with rage at the man's words, Slocum smashed Tarp in the face with his doubled-up fist and knocked him flat on his back.

"Both of you get your boots off. I'm going to teach you two a lesson you won't forget. Shed everything but your pants and be damn quick about it."

"What—what for?" Napier stuttered, then seeing the anger written on Slocum's face, hurried to obey and undressed.

Slocum fashioned a reata around each of their necks in a chain fashion, and nodded to Amy, who was by then sitting her horse. "I'm going to deliver them to the citizens of Oxbow and see how they like these two ambushers."

She gave him a grim nod in agreement, and then they started down the dry wash for the road with his prisoners in tow.

"Keep up or be drug," he said to them while riding up to join her.

In a short while, the two were staggering behind, moaning

about the stickers in their feet and how they needed a drink. Slocum only looked back and scowled at them. "You've got two choices, shut up or die."

They chose the former. At last on the road, he pushed Red into a long walk. They reach Oxbow in mid-afternoon, and the curious came out of the store and saloon to see what they'd brought them this time.

"Is there someone here can send word to Yates for him to come down here and rescue his back-shooters? I'm tying them to that cottonwood tree, and I don't want anyone to cut them loose but the old man." He dropped out of the saddle. Looking at a barefoot boy in his early teens, he said, "Go in the store and get me a hundred feet of hemp rope."

The boy took off on a dead run. Slocum turned back to his prisoners, who were sitting on the ground moaning and pulling stickers out of their bare, dirty, bleeding feet.

"Stand up," he ordered.

"You going to hang us?" Tarp asked.

"I should, but not now. Stand up. I am going to tie your hands behind your backs and then string you up under that tree to wait for your boss to come cut you loose. And I want you to tell him, when he comes after me, the rope will be around his neck, not his wrists. Hear me?"

"Tell him you'll lynch him if—he—comes after you?"

"Tell him 'cause I'm tired of his harassment of this lady." He tossed his head toward Amy. "He needs better manners."

Someone brought them a pail of water and a dipper for a drink. Slocum threw the rope over the thick branch, and tied them so their arms were over their heads and they had to stand on the ground or swing from their arms. The crowd across the dusty street had been quiet and stayed over there, talking under their breath among themselves while watching him get the two men set up.

His job completed, he motioned to Amy that he wanted go get a bottle of whiskey at the saloon.

"Mister, you just leaving them two there like that?" a young man asked.

"Damn right I am, and anyone else who tries to bush-whack us will get like punishment. I want their boss to cut them down if he ever comes."

The man swallowed hard. "They could die there."

Slocum looked back and shook his head. "They won't. But they can think about being a hired gun for a long while there and the things that can happen to them."

"Yes, sir."

"You certainly don't have many Christian ways about you, sir," the same graying-haired woman who chewed him out last time said.

"No, ma'am. But those two don't either."

She snorted, threw her shawl over her shoulder, and stalked off.

Slocum got his whiskey, and walked out the saloon door into the bright sunlight. Amy held out his reins to him and he took them, putting the bottle in his saddlebags and swinging his leg over the saddle. He nodded to everyone there. "Until the next time."

They rode off.

"That won't stop Yates," she said, looking off toward Four Peaks as they rode south.

He hunched up in the sharp wind out of the north. Turning colder. Some thin-looking high clouds had moved in. "No, but it will rattle his men. Those two will pack and ride. They won't walk for years without one of those stickers jabbing them as a reminder. If they're smart, they'll find a new line of work."

"How many more can he have?"

"I figure he'll send Yonken next."

"Yonken. Him and Ernie had a fight one time in Oxbow. It ended in a draw and both of them were bloody. Oh, I was upset enough to want to gun Yonken down that day. Ernie said no."

"I won't fight him with my fists. These two got the easy treatment today."

She nodded, shaking out a blanket to wrap in against the growing cold.

"Good idea, girl. I've been freezing for the last hour."

"Should we go back to the cave?"

He nodded. "But first we better check and see if Marshal Hendren has been by your place and left a note."

She agreed as he loosened a blanket of his own from his bedroll to use for a coat. It was growing colder by the minute.

Huddled under their blankets an hour later, they checked the ramada and found nothing. So they headed back for their hideout taking a wide loop. Clouds had thickened and light snow had begun to fall as they gained altitude. The steep trails were almost slick with a coating by the time they neared the cave, and then even their shod horses slipped a little in a place or two.

At last inside, he took the horses and she worked on starting a fire. In the cavern and out of the wind and cold precipitation, he shed his blanket. He unsaddled and fed the horses grain in nose bags, then found the packhorse was there too waiting for his share. Slocum fed him as well. Then he went to join Amy as flames licked up through her split logs.

"Snow is not a regular thing here," she said.

"Ah, into everyone's life some snow should fall."

"I've personally had enough bad things in my life. Oh, I just wish Ernie was out of jail."

He knelt down beside her and hugged her. "I think the governor will get to the bottom of it in time."

She turned and kissed him. Then she hung her chin on his shoulder and shook her head, "I sure miss Ernie so much, until there are days I think I'll go crazy if he doesn't come home soon."

"We'll figure it out. If Sterling can't get him out, there has to be other means like asking a judge for a retrial."

She squeezed him. "I hope you realize what a friend you've been to me. Being out here alone in all this, I might have committed suicide."

"Don't you ever think that way. No matter what, life is good and the sun will shine in yours one day."

She pushed him back. "I won't. I know how hard things have been for you, being hounded by bounty hunters all these years. If you can stand it, I can, too, and I always will." Then, with a look of mischief, she kissed him again. "It would be warmer and much better under the covers."

"Hey, whatever. Let me check things first and I'll be back. You warm up the covers."

Snowflakes swirled at the entrance doing a great dance, like a million moths. The horses were calm and half asleep, standing hipshot inside the shelter. Horses could detect things like someone approaching long before a man could. He used their powers all the time for protection. Satisfied, he went back up into the cavern and stoked the fire. Then he undid his gun belt, shed his britches and shirt, and hurried under the blankets with the cold air rushing over him.

Her warm silky skin against his own made him swallow hard when he slipped under the covers to lay beside her. His hand ran over her hard-muscled stomach, and his fingers slipped through her wiry pubic hair. Her legs spread apart for him, and he began to tease her clit with the tip of his index finger until it began to stiffen and she shifted nervously under his touch.

"Oh, damn," she swore, then swallowed hard and threw her head back. Her fingers closed on his. "Take me. Take me, please."

He moved between her legs, and she pulled the covers over them. His turgid dick slid inside her wet lubricated gates, and she raised her butt off the bedroll to accept him, gasping for her breath. With the entry complete, he began pounding her hard. Contractions began deep inside her, adding to the excitement as they became more and more frenzied. Her bare heels spurred the back of his legs, and she hunched at his every probe until they fell into a breath-stealing whirlpool.

His left testicle felt as if it was in a vise, and he fought to relieve it. The head of his dick was swollen so tight, it felt ready to split apart any second and explode. On and on they went. Her clit was so stiff, it felt like a sharpened stick scratching on the top of his erection.

"Get up on your hands and knees," he whispered.

She nodded, looking excited. He reared back to give her room to turn over, and then he moved against her hard butt and she slid his aching dick into her wet cunt.

With a gasp, she pushed into him. He reached underneath her, and when his fingers found her swollen clit, she gulped hard at his actions and then cried out loud, "Dear God." And soon she fainted, facedown, in a pile.

He rolled her over and smiled at her. Pushing his still-rock-hard dick inside her, he soon awoke her, and he felt the rise from his screaming testicles as he shoved his pubic bone hard against hers. The explosion threatened to split the head of his prick apart. Then, he came all over again in a great spasmodic explosion, depleting all the muscles in his butt.

Connected, they slept naked in each other's arms until sundown. She woke, dressed, made a fire, and began boiling water for coffee. Dry-eyed, he came around, rose, put on his clothes, and went to check on things at the entrance. Still snowing. The flakes were drier than earlier, but the accumulation on the ground was several inches.

"Heckuva of a snow out there for this country," he said, and came back to warm up by her fire.

"Unusual," she agreed. "But like always, we can use the moisture. Besides, it'll make the spring flowers. I wonder how much this'll put off things for us."

"No telling. It won't last long."

"No, the sun will melt it fast. What can we do today?"

"Cover some more ground. No telling what else Yates is up to toward the others."

"There might be some mail from the governor in town."

"Might, but he sounded like he had to do lots of investigating first."

She looked up from her cooking and shrugged at him, sweeping the hair back from her face. "We could go back to bed."

"That ain't an altogether bad idea."

With a pot holder, she picked up the coffeepot and came over to where he sat on the ground. "Coffee first. Then some food. Maybe Nick Thomas knows something. I haven't talked to him in weeks. He's a neighbor lives west closer to the Verde."

"We can check on all that today. You need any supplies?"

"Sure, always can use something."

"Better take our bedrolls in case we get caught out tonight."

"Two of them would look more respectable. I sure don't know what I'd've done without you." She laughed while serving him hashed-brown potatoes and fried bacon.

She sat cross-legged beside him with her own plate.

The north wind was sharp when they mounted up to leave. They used blankets to wrap in for extra warmth, and they reached Nick Thomas's place in mid-morning. A white-bearded man stuck a rifle barrel out of the tent flap. "That you, Mrs. Branch?"

"It's me and a friend, Nick."

"Get in here. It's colder than blue blazes out there."

They hitched their horses and Slocum ducked, following her inside. The man, in his fifties, had lit a candle lamp. He came over and hugged Amy.

"Been hearing you two been giving Yates lots of hell."

She introduced Slocum. While the men shook hands, she pulled off her gloves and warmed her hands at the large sheet-iron stove in the center of the tent.

"Glad to meet you," said Nick. "Any friend of her and Ernie's is a friend of mine. You two been causing a stir down at Oxbow." He laughed and showed them to some folding canvas chairs. "Sit a spell and tell me all you know."

"Guess we can start telling you about our Prescott trip," she said, and looked at Slocum for reassurance.

Hell, yes. He nodded for her to continue. Her friend needed to know everything.

8

"I sure hope it works. I mean, I hope it clears the whole thing up about Ernie being framed and cleans up that bunch down at Globe," Nick said to the two of them. "I've got some beef hanging. I'll go cut some off and we'll have supper a little early."

"We can help you," Amy said.

"You ain't run into Yonken again, have you?" the older man asked Slocum.

"You heard about that?"

"It was the talk of the town down at the saloon. Anyone who's stood up to Yonken and survived is a hero around here."

They all three laughed. Not an easy laugh, but more to relieve some of the tension that hung in the air inside the tent. Nick went outside to cut some meat off the carcass hanging on a cross arm. Opening the tent flap, Slocum looked around at the gray world outside, saw nothing out of place, and then closed it.

"Nick's a good man," she said, busy peeling potatoes.

"Yes, he is." Opening the tent flap again, Slocum watched Nick recovering the beef with the tarp and then heading back.

Nick came inside with the meat. "I figure Yates and his bunch are denned up with this bad weather. But he'll be a hard man to ever contain."

"Maybe we can make him realize we're serious. I would like to meet Yates face to face," Slocum said.

"Probably get you shot in the back," Nick said, busy slicing off slabs of meat with a sharp knife.

"I think so, too," Amy said. "Ernie tried to talk to him, and look where it got him."

"Wait around Oxbow and he's liable to show up any day," Nick said.

"I've missed him the times I've been there," Slocum said.

"Yeah, you missed his cussing over your poor treatment of his hired thugs."

"Any of them stay around after that?"

"No, you been cleaning them out." Nick slapped the meat on the table. He was ready to flour it for frying. "His bunkhouse is probably about empty. They've been drifting out of here all right. But he's a rattler, and you've stirred him up plenty enough to have him striking mad."

"Good."

"You just better watch. That Yonken is a drygulcher, and they tell me another bad one drifted in this week named Farnam."

"Chelsey Farnam." Amy put her fingers over her mouth in shock.

"He's the one Yates hired to rape her," Slocum said. "Don't worry he won't get another chance."

"I'm sorry, Amy. I never knew a damn thing about that or I'd've cut his heart out." Nick slammed the big knife on the table.

"Farnam and some others attacked her with masks," Slocum explained. "She recognized his big voice on the street when we went to Prescott." He gestured to Amy to tell her side of it.

"I reported it down in Globe," she said, "and they said I'd need names to swear out a warrant."

"They got sorry excuses for lawmen down there. What can I do?"

"Be on the lookout for U.S. Marshal Sam Hendren. He's coming over here on behalf of the governor to look this situation over and do what he can."

"Can he do anything?" Nick asked, busy dredging the steaks in flour to prepare them to fry.

Slocum nodded. "We have to have faith that he can. Maybe call a grand jury and investigate it all."

"That would beat what we have gotten done for sure. I've never felt more helpless in my entire life than when they framed Ernie and sent him to prison. Nothing a man can do when the law is that crooked."

Amy poured them each cups of coffee. "It's been some rough months," she said.

"I know, Amy, but I didn't know what to do."

"It wasn't your fault, Nick."

He shook his head and then stoked the stove under his second skillet. Her sliced potatoes were in the other skillet sizzling away.

They spent the night with Nick, and after breakfast in the cold dawn, they rode into Oxbow. Snow clung to everything, even on top of the tall arms of the saguaros. It was a white land, with the Four Peaks looking like four ice cream cones. Slocum and Amy came off the south hillside into the small village, and hitched at the store. She went inside to get a few supplies, and he crossed over to the Irish Saloon to talk to Tommy Burke and have a drink.

"Well, well, Slocum you look no worse for wear," the man said to him with a smile from behind the bar. "You've been awfully hard on some of the ranch hands around here lately. Awfully hard. Hurting my business."

"Sorry about that," Slocum said, raising the whiskey glass.

"Slocum! Slocum!" He could hear Amy screaming. He set the glass down, grabbed for his gun butt, and rushed out in the snowy street looking both ways for trouble. Halfway across the street he holstered his gun and caught her in his arms.

"They—they—killed Ernie in Yuma."

"Oh, my God. Who did?" Then he noticed that she'd fainted, and he swept her up in his arms. He looked around, and decided the saloon might be the place to take her. He went inside the wooden doors. The batwings were tied back, and the real doors were now used to block out the cold.

"What's wrong?" Tommy asked, looking at Amy and acting upset.

"Ernie's dead, she said. Must be the letter out in the street. She dropped it."

"I'll go get it."

"Where can I put her?"

Tommy waved him toward the rear. "Put her on my bed in the back room. I'll go get you that letter."

"Yes, I need to read it."

What else would happen? Ernie dead? He could hardly believe it had happened.

Amy revived on the bed, sobbing. Slocum turned the page to the light coming in the four-panel window.

Dear Mrs. Branch,

This letter is to inform you that your husband Ernie Branch, prisoner number 4587, was murdered in a prison riot by inmates unknown five days ago. #4587 was stabbed several times in the back while trying to protect the lives of two guards. His efforts to save the guards succeeded, but he lost his own life in the process.

He will be pardoned of all his crimes and was buried last week in a real grave in the St. Thomas Cemetery in Yuma. Through a collection drive, a headstone will be placed on the grave site to recognize his bravery.

There is nothing I can do to console you in your

sorrow and loss, but I will say, no braver man ever lived than Ernie Branch.

Warden John Clay
Yuma Territorial Prison
Yuma, A.T.

Wet-faced, she sat up on the cot. "What will I do, Slocum? What will I do without him?"

"Go on fighting. That's what he'd expect."

She stopped her trembling and sniffling to agree with a nod. "Yes. He'd—want it that way."

"Damn right." He hugged her tight. *What will happen next?*

9

Through his brass telescope, Slocum studied the Yates ranch headquarters. Squatted on his heels in the cover of the brushy juniper boughs, he could make out the horses and hay. Smoke was rising from a tin chimney, and the snow was beginning to melt a drop at a time off the eaves and tips of branches in the bright sun.

"See anything?" she asked, creeping up beside him.

"No one's came out since I got here, besides the cook, who came outside for an armload of cooking wood."

"Reckon Yates is home?"

"I imagine so. I have not heard of him leaving the country since I got here—whoa, we have company." He turned, and saw the tears streaming down Amy's face.

"I'm sorry, Slocum. I just can't—get over his death."

"I know. I know, and he wouldn't have been there if these worthless people hadn't framed him. Sheriff Cummings and another man just rode up."

"Let me see." She took the glass from him. "That's that no-good Scroggins."

"Wonder what they want."

"Probably to collect more money, don't you think?"

"To get Cummings up here, I'd say it was damn important business."

"How will we find out?"

"Wait and see, I'm afraid. Maybe Marshal Hendren has things afoot in Globe."

Fifteen minutes later, Amy was still looking through the glass. "There's two hands coming out and going to the corral," she said. She handed him back the glass.

"We'll intercept them and see what's happening," he said.

She made a wry face at him. "Reckon they'll tell us anything?"

"They know how we handled the others. I doubt they want that kind of treatment." He closed down the scope and waited to see which way the two rode off.

The two hands headed south all hunched down in their saddles against the cold despite the sun's attempt to warm things. Slocum chuckled to himself. They'd sure not be happy ranch hands, getting shut out in the cold.

Half an hour later, Slocum and Amy rode out of the junipers up a canyon, each holding a rifle on the two.

"Don't move an inch 'less you want a funeral in this slush."

"You Slocum?" The younger one blinked in disbelief.

"Hush up, kid," the older one said.

"No, kid, talk all you want. Get off your horses and start getting undressed."

"You ain't going to—"

"Going to what? Make you two go back to the ranch barefooted and with only your pants on? Is that what you're asking?"

"Yeah."

Slocum nodded several times in agreement, and then he looked back in the direction of the ranch headquarters. "Ain't over two or three miles back, is it?"

"Why, we'll freeze to death, and the damn stickers."

"Well, tell me why Cummings and his deputy are up here." Slocum looked hard at the older one.

"I guess a social visit. The old man contributes to his re-election."

"No. He came on more serious business than that."

"You know so damn much, go ask him."

Slocum leveled the rifle at him. "Start undressing."

"Wait," the kid said. "He came to tell the old man there was going to be a grand jury. I heard that. Then Yates told us to go check the poisoned springs."

"You hear that?" Slocum pointed his rifle at the older man.

"Yeah, something like that. Then Yates shut Cummings up. He told us we had to go check the springs."

"You hear the name Hendren?"

The kid nodded at Amy. "That sumbitch Hendren is behind it all were the words I heard."

Slocum nodded at Amy. She acknowledged it with a grim set to her mouth.

With the rifle across his lap, Slocum told the two to stop undressing. "You've got two options. Ride right on to Fort McDowell and out of this country, or undress."

"You mean clear out?" the old man said.

"Yes, ride out of here and don't come back."

"What if we go get our things?"

"It'll be barefooted."

He nodded. "Guess we're out of here," he said to the kid.

"I was going even if you weren't," the kid said.

"How many more hands are left?" Slocum asked.

"The old man and Yonken. Two gunhands rode in from across the Salt River the other night, and they said something about you two weren't coming down there. They demanded their money and left."

"What did Yates say to that?"

"He cussed some, but said that there was a hundred better ones than them to hire."

Slocum stuck his rifle in the boot. "Be sure it ain't you two."

"I won't be back, and I'm sure the kid won't either."

"Hell, no, I won't be back in this country again. I took a

drink out of one of those poison springs before we knew they'd been poisoned, and I figured I'd die."

Slocum nodded, trying not to let his amusement show.

Dressed, the two hands rode off to the southwest for the main road. Slocum and Amy watched them and when they were out of hearing, Slocum and Amy chuckled with each other.

"Poor boy thought he'd die 'cause we planted that sign," she said with a snicker.

"I mean, he was ready to cash in his chips."

She closed her eyes and dropped her chin. "What next?"

"We better check and see if Hendren is around here. He's supposed to leave word at the ramada."

"I hope he's coming, but Slocum—if I ever needed being rocked to sleep, I'll damn sure need it tonight."

"I know what you mean. I've tried to keep you busy so your mind was off it—but I understand your hurting."

Tears flooded her face. "I can't help it."

He rode over and hugged her. "I know we both lost a great friend."

"Those bastards Yates and Cummings."

"We'll get 'em. They'll pay. Hendren has them on the run, I think."

She closed her wet eyes and shook her head. "Oh, God. I hope so."

So did he.

10

There was no sign of Hendren having been at the ramada. Slocum fed the horses. Meanwhile, Amy built a fire in the stove. The wind blew hard, and when he returned to the stove, the heat from her blaze felt good.

"Reckon Hendren's even coming?" she asked.

"Yes. If he's having a grand jury, he'll be needing testimony from you."

"What will this jury do?"

"The grand jury'll listen to the testimony and decide who needs to stand trial. The prosecutor will have them charged with crimes. Have them arrested and tried in court for that crime."

"But—but he was in on poor Ernie's prosecution."

Slocum agreed. "Hendren may have him on the stand."

She broke into tears. "Slocum, Slocum, I didn't even get to attend his funeral."

He held her tight against his chest and felt her sobbing. Each time, it was like a knife in his heart. Later, they ate supper, and then they crawled in to the bedroll with him holding her in a ball against his stomach. It was hard for him to fall asleep. Somewhere off in the night, a red wolf howled and his mate answered.

His erection began to blossom with her familiar butt stuck to him, and he eased himself lower behind her to get in position. Then, with gentle care he slipped it inside her gates. She reached back and felt the side of his bare leg and as if satisfied, pushed herself back at him with his entry deeper into her cunt.

Soon, she rolled over on her belly and took him with her. On hands and knees with her face on the bedding, she began to hunch against him, breathing harder and harder, until she threw her head back and strained. He felt her faint in a pile under him. Good, maybe after that she could really sleep.

They soon slept. But the night turned into a horrific whirlpool. Someone was kicking him in the ribs, and he couldn't roll out of the blankets. The last thing Slocum remembered was hearing her scream. Then his lights went out.

It was past sunup when he awoke. Groggy, with a pounding headache, and about to freeze, he raised up on his hands and knees. His bare skin felt like ice as he groped around. He couldn't see his handgun anywhere in sight. Where was Amy and who took her? Sumbitch! This was serious, and he was so beat up he couldn't hardly do more than crawl. Someone had used his body for a kicking bag—that would heal in time. It was Amy that he worried the most about.

Finally, his breath catching from time to time, he managed to get dressed. Then, wrapped in a blanket and shivering half to death, he found one of the rifles he and Amy had brought along. So at last, he possessed a gun. A horse would be next. There were none in sight. The attackers had either stolen the hobbled horses or run them off. Being afoot was close to being unarmed in this country. He bent over from the sharp pains in his side. Whoever did this to him better have on his funeral suit 'cause he was going to pay with his life.

No sign of Red or the other two horses. He better head for Oxbow. There was jerky in the panniers. He found the long-tail canvas duster. He stuffed the pockets with jerky and raisins, then thought about shells for a .44/40. He'd sure need them if he found the kidnappers.

Half a box of cartridges was all he could locate. He

checked the sun time. Around noon. His head was pounding so hard, he knew it was why his vision was blurred. He swept up his hat off the ground and headed for town.

All he could think about was how he must look like a drunk staggering around as he headed north for Oxbow. The sharp rocks would eat up his rundown boots by the time he reached the village, but there was nothing he could do about that. He had to press on.

"You all right, mister?"

He tried to see the bearer of the youthful voice. The sun's rays blinded him, and all he could make out was an outline. "I will be—in a minute or two."

"It was a wonder someone didn't run over you. You were all passed out in the middle of the road."

His mouth was so dry, his tongue tried to stick to its roof. He nodded. Then a deep hacking cough cut off his wind. His mind swirled, and next he knew, he was lying on the bed of a light wagon and the driver was racing it somewhere—maybe to hell. He was sliding around corners and hitting washouts on the fly.

"Hold up," Slocum finally managed to say loud enough for the driver to hear him.

"You come to again?" the boy asked, reining in his team.

"Yes. A jog will do."

"Sure. Sure. I thought you'd die on me. My name's Agee. Dwight Agee."

"Slocum's mine."

"I heard about you bringing Yates's men in barefooted to town. They do this to you?"

"Someone did—right now, I don't know who to thank for it."

The boy laughed. "I wouldn't be thanking them, sir."

"If I get the chance, I'll thank them all right."

Lying on his back in the wagon, Slocum knew one thing— it was close to sundown when they pulled up in Oxbow. In minutes, men rushed out of the Irish Saloon and carried him in to the back room. Tommy Burke supervised the operation.

"Who did this to ya?" They must have asked him that a thousand times.

"I was asleep. They kidnapped Mrs. Branch is all I know right now."

"Kidnapped Ernie's wife? Why, them sons a bitches. How many were there?" The questions went on and on until Tommy ordered all of the men outside the room.

"You rest a while," Tommy said.

"I need a horse and a six-gun . . . "

"You don't need shit right now, me friend," he told Slocum. "Rest. Why, a damn mouse could kick your legs out from under you. You're safe here. Could we learn anything about where they took Mrs. Branch if we rode out there?"

"A good Indian tracker might find his tracks."

"I'll send for one from Fort McDowell."

"We were at her ranch headquarters when it happened. I was sure sleeping when they started pounding and kicking me—then they hit me over the head and it all went blank."

"Here, drink some whiskey. Then rest. Some of us will handle it from here on."

Propped up on an elbow, he took a deep swallow from the glass, and the liquor cut a hot path down his throat. It might in time ease the pain. He handed the glass back and dropped back on the bed. "Thanks. She don't deserve this."

"I know. I know." Tommy covered him up.

Dreams danced through his brain. Not dreams about grassy meadows and clear streams bubbling through them—these murals were battle scenes. Cannon fire and exploding bombs, wild cav charges against impenetrable lines of smoking rifles. His teeth clenched as he heard the screams of dying men all around him. Then he awoke in a cold sweat, and realized those screams were his own.

"You all right?" Tommy stood with his head stuck in the doorway.

Slocum nodded. "Old battles—dreams."

"I sent for some trackers to meet us at Mrs. Branch's place in the morning."

"Thanks. I'll try to be more quiet."

"Don't worry about it. Get some rest."

His bladder woke him with an urgency, and he was shocked to see a woman in the room busy knitting with a small lamp on a side table. "Can I get you anything?" she asked.

Slocum shook his head. "Just excuse me for a minute."

Pain shot to his brain and he gritted his teeth. When he was on his feet, she opened the door, and he stepped down the hall and outside under the stars. The cold wind swept his face. Funny thing. He could not remember what the woman in the room had looked like. Pissing off in to the darkness, he wondered about Amy. Where had her captors taken her? Who were they? Short of a miracle, he'd not be able to ride with the trackers.

He went back inside, and the woman was at the lighted doorway in the hall. "I was getting worried about you."

Closing the back door, he nodded at her, and noticed the saloon must be closed for the night. "I'm all right. A little light-headed is all. I'm hoping I can join the posse in the morning."

The tall slender woman was in her thirties, he guessed. "My name is Hallie. Hallie Greenwood."

"Mrs.?"

"Yes, but call me Hallie."

"Slocum's mine."

"Yes, I have heard all about you. You're a folk hero in the basin these days."

"A dumb one anyway." He was grateful for the short distance to the bed. There was a potbellied stove in the shadowy room, and a stack of split firewood was beside it.

"Are you hungry?" she asked.

"I have no idea." Seated on the edge of the bed, he held his sore face in his hands.

"I have some bean soup on the stove. Would you try some?"

He closed his eyes and dropped his chin. "All I want to do is sleep."

"You can sit up. I'll feed you. You'll need the energy to ever recover."

"You must have children. You sound like my mother."

"Two boys."

"What does your husband do?"

She shook her head. "I'm a widow. He's dead."

"Oh, I'm sorry. I thought—"

"No way you could know. Jim died in a horse wreck last year."

"Must be tough. Being alone up here."

"Folks have been kind. I wanted to hold the ranch together for the boys when they grow up. Yates hasn't made that easy."

"Yates hasn't made anything easy that I can hear about." He watched her swish across the room in the long dress, ladle out some steaming liquid in a bowl, and return.

She took a place sitting beside him on the bed, and he could smell the hint of cinnamon that she wore. Blowing on each spoonful, she fed him as he sat up while fighting the claws trying to pull him back down on the bed.

"Is that enough?" she asked from a distant entrance to the deep cave he resided in.

"Yes—plenty . . . ." His head hit the pillow and exhausted, he fell asleep.

"The saloon's not open today—" There was an urgent sound in her voice that awoke him. It was coming from the open door of the room.

"I want a damn drink open or not. I'll just help myself then."

"No, I said it was closed."

"Get out of the way, bitch!"

Hallie gave a cry, and it was obvious to Slocum in the back room that someone'd pushed her to the floor. He lifted the Winchester that was leaning against the wall and checked the chamber. His vision was still not clear. He heard broken glass.

In he hall, he steadied himself against the wall and looked

toward the light coming in from the barroom. Rifle in his hands, he heard Hallie suck in her breath.

"What I need is a little pussy to go with my whiskey, girl. You got some, honey." Then he laughed aloud. "Where's all these nesters at?"

No answer.

"I been wanting to poke you since the first time I seed ya. Where are they at?"

"Out looking for Amy Branch."

"Where in the hell did she go? That Slocum sumbitch with her?"

"Slocum is right here." He faced the man with the rifle butt against his hip.

Rylie Yonken, wide-eyed, went for the six-gun on his hip. Slocum pointed the barrel at him, and the report of the rifle blast hurt his ears. Through the thick gun smoke, he saw he had hit Yonken and staggered him. But Slocum went blank for a second or two. Next thing he saw, Yonken came up holding Hallie as a shield.

"I'll kill her, too. Drop that rifle."

"Don't listen to him," she said.

Slocum dropped the long gun in the sawdust. Filled with dread, he watched Yonken backing for the doorway with Hallie as his defense. "You follow me, she's dead. Hear me?"

"You hurt her and you'll hang."

"We'll see about that."

"I'll see to it."

Yonken aimed his pistol at Slocum, but when he went to pull the trigger, Hallie shoved his gun hand aside and the bullet struck in a shelf of full bottles. One shattered.

"You bitch—" And he was out the door dragging her with him.

Slocum swept up the rifle. He steadied himself against the wall, drew a deep breath, and staggered as fast as he could for the open front doors.

Once on the porch, he saw Yonken trying to drag Hallie

up over his lap as his horse spooked backward into the street. She fought him like a hellcat. Slocum swallowed hard and used the porch post to steady the rifle. His vision was coming and going as he took aim and fired. His bullet took Yonken in the face, and he spilled off the tail of his horse.

Smoking rifle in his hand, Slocum came straight at Yonken's prone body, shooting him over and over every second step. The lead bullets striking his body sounded like they were hitting a large watermelon.

Hallie at last forced down the rifle, which was clicking on empty as he tried to fire it. "He's dead," she said.

"You're sure?"

"Come on before you pass out on me here in the street."

She had to force him to turn away from the dead man. Pushing him along toward the Irish Saloon, she took the rifle from him. "By God, he won't rape any more women," Slocum said. "He won't beat up any more men. He won't push any more small ranchers around ever again. He's going to roast in hell for eternity."

"Slocum? Are you going to make it? Put your arm on my shoulder. There, lean on me. We don't have far to go. You all right?"

Somehow, she got him back to his room, because hours later he woke wound up under the covers in bed. What was that clicking sound? Her needles, busy knitting. There she sat in the light of the lamp, busy making a sweater, he guessed. Did that woman ever sleep?

"What happened to his body?"

"It's in the back of the store. A couple of men rode by and they carried him over there. Why worry about him?"

He shook his head. "I have no idea. Just was worried— concerned, hell, I don't know."

She came over with a bowl of steaming soup and took her place beside him on the bed. "It was damn good riddance."

"You hear anything from the posse?"

"No word."

"I should be up there helping them."

"Oh, yes, and fall off your horse." She held up the spoon to feed him. "What could you do that they can't?"

"They're not manhunters."

"And you are."

"Sorry I shot him so many times."

"I wasn't. He deserved every bullet he received and some more."

"I must be getting better. I can taste the soup now."

She smiled with pride. "That sounds wonderful. Maybe you are recovering."

He closed his eyes. He certainly hoped so.

11

Under a blanket in the morning sunshine, Slocum sat in a rocker on the Irish Saloon's front porch. He could see the weary-looking posse returning on their jaded horses. No Amy in sight either. That sight knifed him deep in his gut.

Tommy dropped out of the saddle and handed the reins to another. "Put him up and thank Mr. Cain for letting me use him."

The saloon owner stopped at the base of the porch. He raised his face and looked up at Slocum. "We never found her."

"Where did they take her?"

"Those trackers looked high and low. The snow melting didn't help. Some think they rode off to the west. Others thought that was a false trail."

"Any idea who took her?"

"No. It's like the earth swallowed them up."

Slocum closed his eyes. Still sore and weak, he thought about where he could look for her. Maybe he'd find the old prospector Rufus McClain. If anyone knew anything, Rufus might. He'd sure defend Amy, and be mad as hell that anyone had harmed a hair on her head.

"You tried hard," Slocum said. "You need some rest. Besides, you lost a customer while you were gone."

Tommy blinked at him. "Who was that?"

"Yonken. He came busting in and shoved Hallie around over you being closed. Must have been drunk. He's over in the back of the store."

Tommy glanced across the street. "No big loss to anyone but Yates."

"He ain't been here. They sent word to him over a day ago."

"Maybe he don't care either. I better open up. I owe some drinks to some of the men who helped me."

Slocum agreed.

Hallie came to the doorway and smiled at the two of them. "Have any luck?"

"No, ma'am." Tommy shook his head as if to clear it.

"They can't just disappear."

"They have for now."

"That's very sad." She chewed on her lower lip, and then quickly disappeared back inside.

Tommy raised his eyebrows and shot a questioning gaze at Slocum.

"She's been through lots around here. The Yonken deal was real bad. I didn't help it either."

"You feeling better?"

"If I don't have to wrestle a pissant, I'll be fine."

They both laughed.

Slocum shifted the wool blanket over himself again. The six-gun, smelling of new gun oil, rested in his lap under the covers. He wasn't taking any chances. No telling how Yates would take the demise of his foreman. Besides, Slocum had little use for the man anyway. It wouldn't take much of an excuse to shoot him for what he did to Ernie.

How could Slocum have handled this business better? No way he could have kept Ernie alive with him behind the Yuma walls. Maybe he should have treed Yates sooner.

"I have some lunch ready. Come eat with us," Hallie said from the doorway.

"Thanks," he said, looking around before rising.

He stuck the new .44 in his waistband and draped the blanket over his arm as he went back inside. Where in hell's name would he start looking for Amy? Maybe the cavern up on Four Peaks.

Two days later, Slocum started out leading a long-legged paint packhorse and riding a short bay mountain pony. Hallie had packed him some food in with the store items. The horses were on loan from her sons, who brought them in from the ranch. Johnny and Star, ages sixteen and eighteen, were anxious to join him in the search.

"Aw, you two have ranch work to do. Besides your mother might skin me."

"You need us, you know where we're at," Star said with a hard set to his jaw. "And Bollie is the best horse we own. Don't worry about his size. He's all bottom and grit."

"Thanks. I'll take good care of him."

"Paw'd've been proud you were riding him," Star said with a nod of approval. "We hope you get those kidnappers and get her back safely."

He shook their hands, thanked them again, and set out for the south. The day acted like it would warm up, and he felt grateful for it. How far could he ride? He still felt he was running at half speed.

At the ramada, he searched around the place. Red wasn't around, nor was the packhorse—they must have been taken out of the country. No message from Marshal Hendren either. Slocum rode on up the mountain, hoping to be at the cave by sundown.

Six-gun in hand, he searched the cave's interior with the candle lamp—no sign that anyone had been there since the last time he and Amy had spent the night there. He'd hoped that they'd've been there—it left him few other places to search, save for Yates's outfit itself.

Rufus arrived about sundown, his burro braying at Slocum's horses.

Rufus held his worn-out hat over his heart. "Damn, I'm sorry about Amy—Mrs. Branch. You haven't found her, have you?"

"No, and I have no leads. No one knows a thing about who took her or what they did with her. Come have some coffee. I've about run out of places to search. The Yavapai trackers couldn't make sense out of the tracks, the snow melting and all."

"You never knowed who it was, huh?"

"No, I woke up that night with someone kicking hell out of me, and then they must of whacked me over the head. I didn't come to for hours, and they were gone when I came to and so were the horses."

"Sounds like when they killed that cowboy and raped her."

"I guess you're right, but two of his men are dead. Chelsey Farnam had never even entered my mind." What had those cowboys or someone said—Yates hired Chelsey Farnam.

"Didn't they arrested that Farnam fella over at Prescott?" Rufus asked.

Slocum had gone for the coffeepot, and poured some for the old man. "I'm not sure about that."

"I never knew his name before, but you told me about the run-in you two had in Prescott with him."

"If he took her, he was liable to take her back toward Prescott."

"He sure might have."

"I've scoured this country, and so did the posse. But Tommy never mentioned going west across the Verde to look for her."

Rufus blew on the steam over his cup. "There's lots of country over in Bloody Basin to look for them."

"I guess that's where I'll go look next."

"Be careful. That one's figured he caved your head in for good, and he might want to finish the job."

"I will. You ain't seen a U.S. marshal named Hendren, have you?"

"No, but I understand he's been raising hell with them devils down in Globe."

Slocum nodded. "You know they killed Ernie in a prison uprising?"

"I heard about that, too. Understand he saved two guards. Be just like him."

"She'd just found that out."

Rufus dropped his whiskered face. "That's a big shame, too."

Lots of shame going around. He'd be on his way to Bloody Basin before the sun came up. All he worried about was that she was all right.

Late afternoon the next day he forded the Verde and made camp in the bottoms, building a fire to cook some food. When he had water boiling, he added the coffee to it. It would be a cold frosty night, and he regretted not having Amy's warm body to cuddle with in their blankets. Lots of things about her he regretted not having—mainly her company. There were women, and there were women who got along well with a man out in the field. Amy was in the last group—half tomboy competitor and still all woman.

He could recall running his palms over every muscle in her body. Her spirit sent shock waves into him. The rise and fall of her solid breasts underneath him, and her excited clinging response to his lovemaking. Damn—she had to be all right.

In the predawn, he hovered over his small fire reheating coffee and stirring some oats in boiling water for his breakfast. He wanted something to stick to him and warm him up as well.

He broke camp as the sun's first spears came over the distant Mazatzalans. Bollie had a fast swinging walk that Slocum appreciated, and the packhorse kept up. Rather than head west for Prescott, he set out up the river looking for any sign.

No reason for Farnam to head into town. He was wanted there—but he might have a camp or shack somewhere in this broken country that filled this basin. A tough land of prickly pear beds and junipers, deep ravines and plenty of places to ambush a man. There was lots of grass, and since the Apache trouble there was settled, several folks had moved in to set up ranching operations, but the land was so vast, there weren't many in any one place.

Mid-morning, he found an outfit with corrals and a canvas-covered adobe jacal. A short woman came out holding her hand against the low winter sun to look at him. She looked young and bewildered.

"Howdy, ma'am," he said taking off his hat for her. "Is your man about the place?"

"Naw, he's out checking cows," she drawled. "What kin I do fur you?"

"I'm looking for a man about forty. Big man, loud deep voice."

Still shading her eyes with the side of her hand, she shook her head. "You be the first one come by here in months."

"I'm looking for a stout roan horse, too."

"Would he be running loose with a bobtail horse?"

"You seen them?"

"No, but Calvin Dean seen 'em last week."

"Where were they?" Those had to be his ponies.

"Salad Springs, about ten miles north of here."

"Can I ride north and find it?"

"I figure so. Kind a rough country, but every cow track leads to the water hole. You got a wife, mister?"

"No I don't."

"Have ya got a ranch closer to town than this one?"

"I don't own a ranch. You thinking about leaving your husband?"

"He ain't my husband. He's my brother, and my chances of finding a man up here ain't real good. You know what I mean?"

"I do. What's your name?"

"Dana Ruth. Why? You know someone's needing a wife?"

"My name's Slocum, and I'll be watching out for a good one to send up here."

"Well, Slocum, I'd sure be beholding to you."

He tipped his hat to her and booted Bollie northward. If Red was up there, he might find out more about Amy's whereabouts.

Damn, this was vast country. Despite all else, he was proud of the mountain pony he rode. Those boys did well to loan the gelding to him. Maybe in another day, he'd find Red and that would lead him to Amy.

Oh, and he'd need to find Dana Ruth a man, too.

12

He made a dry camp at sundown, hobbled his horses, and wondered if this Salad Springs was a figment of Dana Ruth's imagination. He'd have to give it another day or so. But when he wrapped up in his blankets, he wondered if Amy was really up there and if he could ever find her.

Mid-morning the next day, he discovered a low-walled cabin tucked in a hillside. Could have been there a long time. But the horse biscuits were not that old. The walls were made of adobe and rocks. It looked like a fortress. The latch string was new, and he ducked the lintel going inside. There had been a recent fire in the fireplace, and some dirty tin dishes were on the dry sink. But he searched the building's interior, and there was no evidence Amy had ever been there. Nothing.

He decided to leave the packhorse hobbled there and circle the country. Using his brass telescope, he spotted some movement on the far mountainside. The sight in the glass of his roan horse and the bobtail packhorse one made his heart race. Where was Amy's big bay? Salad Springs must be close at hand. He swung up on Bollie and set out to gather his horses. Turning and twisting in the saddle, he kept an eye out all the time for an ambush.

He crossed a wide dry wash and scaled the far bank. No sign of anyone. He spooked some longhorns and their calves out of the brush. But his goal was to collect his ponies. Juniper boughs brushed his chaps, and he had to rein Bollie around large patches of pear. The mountain proved steep, and he followed the horses' tracks up the game trail.

The two ponies threw up their heads at his approach. He called to them, and Bob answered him and started toward him. Red followed, and Slocum soon had a lead on Bob.

Certain that Red would follow his companion, Slocum headed back downhill.

Where was she at? Damn—he had his horses, and still no Amy. Disappointed, he headed back for the cabin. If Farnam had taken her anywhere, she'd've escaped him by this time unless he had her shackled. Where could the two of them be?

Hobbling Red in the light of bloody sundown, he realized he knew one thing—that Amy and Farnam had obviously come through there. Straightening, he walked away to the edge of the open meadow to empty his bladder. There he saw some fresh red dirt.

Who'd been digging? Shaking the dew off his dick, he put it away and stepped around the tree. Was he looking at a grave? His heart stopped. It was big enough for one. A shorter person.

He glanced back at the cabin. A hundred yards away maybe. This wasn't a mining operation either. It was a grave, and his stomach began to crawl.

He'd need some tools. Filled with knee-weakening dread, he went back and found a broken-handled shovel and an adze at the cabin. Armed with a candle lamp and some extra candles from his pannier, he went back to the edge of the meadow. The business to exhume whatever was under that dirt would not be one of pleasure—but no one dug holes in this dry land except to hide or bury something. This was not a location for fencing, or even for covering up an outhouse hole.

He was forced to get on his knees to even use his pitiful excuse for a shovel, and the rocks in the soil mix clanged against his tool like a bell ringer. Slowly but surely, he removed the fill until the copper smell of death began to escape the earth and fill his nose. He tied the bandanna from around his neck over his mouth and nose to try and filter part of the stench away. It didn't help that much.

There was a human body buried in this grave. And he felt certain it was her. Damn, oh, damn. He eased his way downward, careful not do any damage to the corpse when he reached it. But the knowledge he had was fast turning his guts to roiling like a barrel full of snakes—rattlesnakes. Then he struck something—stopped digging, and began to carefully expose a hand.

When at last he saw it was hers, he jerked the bandanna down and vomited all over the ground beside the shallow grave.

"Damn you, Chelsey Farnam! I'll kill you with my bare hands!"

Farnam could never hide from him. Tears blurred his vision as he exposed her naked body. Between gagging on the dead smell and fighting his own anger as well as disappointment, he struggled on into the night by candle lamp. Once her body was removed and set aside, he used the adze to deepen the hole, and took it down two more feet, since he had no ladder to climb out of it.

Then he scrambled out and found a blanket to wrap her in. By this time, his nose and mind were so numb, he had no idea who or where he was or why even he was even there. The night cold settled in, and went unnoticed by him as he worked on. Nothing, not even the coyotes howling on the next ridge, entered his mind.

At last, when she was wrapped and placed gently in the deeper grave, he said a short prayer for her deliverance and covered her up. As the last scoop of dirt was piled on her grave, the lamp went out. He stood over the mound, crying over his loss and shivering from the cold. Stumbling back to his camp gear, he found the unopened whiskey bottle in his saddlebags. Wrapped up in a couple of blankets, he sat down on the ground to drink and to try to figure out what he should do next.

At last, he fell asleep, and awoke a few hours later as dawn began to sparkle on the frost-coated dead weeds around him. He ate some stiff jerky, saddled Red, and decided to take Hallie Greenwood's horses back to her. Those boys of hers were especially proud of their father's horse Bollie, a powerful mountain horse he'd enjoyed.

Where in the hell had Chelsey Farnam gone after he'd murdered, and no doubt raped, Amy? Maybe he'd figured no one would discover the grave. More questions than answers. Was Farnam working for Yates? Slocum felt certain that Yates had hired the bastard to rape her the first time, to show her she couldn't fight him. Shame that neither of those two in Prescott had lived to talk. Maybe if he found the fourth one, he'd have more answers.

Still shivering from the cold, he set out with his horses for the Greenwood place. Maybe on the way he'd figure out something.

Past noontime, he was coming down a broad dry wash headed for the Verde River when a rifle shot roared through the countryside. Red, in a hard trot, flinched underneath him, and then fell to his front knees and skidded with a grunt to a stop. Some bastard had shot his horse. The other horses traveling loose with him and Red, upset by the sound of the rifle shot, fled the wash. Slocum quickly took cover behind Red's body, waiting for another round to come in.

Why shoot Red, or had they aimed to kill *him*? On his belly behind the dead gelding's body, he tried to listen for any sounds of the shooter or his movements. But nothing was heard. Gradually, he worked up his nerve and removed his own rifle from the scabbard. Then, with a grim shake of his head at his dead mount, he looked around at the countryside in front of him.

The shot had come from the right. It had to have been made off the ridge above him, or he'd've heard the shooter leaving. Determined to find some evidence, he climbed the steep slope and began to look for tracks. At last, he found where a horse had been hitched and had stomped around impatiently. Then, on the ridge, he discovered a copper cartridge; it was long-range sniper ammo for a Remington needle gun. Obviously, the one using that gun had planned to eliminate him. He'd shot low and a little right of his target. Then he must have left.

No cigarette butts or anything on the ground. The wind had been blowing so by the time Slocum had looked that way, the gun smoke had been gone. This hardly seemed like Farnam. He let others do his killing. Slocum wouldn't put it past Yates to put another killer on his trail. Who would Slocum look for next?

No sign of his horses. Even Bob had left, along with the Greenwood horses. Where was Slocum personally at? At least forty miles from Oxbow, with a little jerky in his saddlebags and one blanket on the saddle tied on behind the cantle. The rest of everything else had left out with Bob and the panniers on his back. Good news like that made him feel real secure. He was in a tight place, and with no easy way out.

From his cut-off bridle reins he made a strap for the rifle and the bedroll. Then he slung the saddlebags over his shoulder, loaded the rest, and headed east. This way was downhill. The other side of the river was uphill, but that was a long ways away.

At sundown, he rested at the west bank of the Verde and considered crossing it. It was near knee deep in some places, but he hoped he'd found the shallowest crossing. On the far side, he would build a fire and dry out. The day's temperature had risen some, but when the sun went down, that little heat would fast evaporate.

No sign of the sharpshooter either. If it wasn't Farnam that shot at him—Slocum sat on his butt and pulled off his boots and socks—then someone had trailed him from across the river. Maybe Dana Ruth or her brother had seen whoever tracked him, and maybe they'd loan him a horse or sell him one.

It was still over thirty miles to Oxbow, but less than ten to their place. He put his socks back on, then his boots. He'd walk a ways downriver, get a few hours' sleep somewhere down there, and arrive at their place after dawn. Rising to his feet, he felt better about that trip than he had about making the crossing and building a fire.

When twilight set in, he unfurled his blanket for a coat and for warmth. The trail was smooth and the rushing sounds of the river were like a song. An owl hooted off in the distance.

About midnight, he denned up in the top of a fallen cottonwood tree for a few hours' sleep. Awakening a few hours later, he resumed his hiking under the stars, until he could hear a rooster crowing over the next rise. A stock dog barked at him when he came down the dusty trail through the junipers toward the jacal.

Dana Ruth stuck her head out the door and squinted at his approach. "Oh, it's Mr. Slocum. He's coming on foot, Calvin Dean."

A lanky bareheaded man close to her age stuck his head out above her. "Why's he coming afoot?"

"I'll ask him."

"'Cause someone shot my good roan horse out from under me yesterday," Slocum said.

"Well, I'll be jiggered. I seen him. He was a helluva horse, mister."

"Slocum."

"Calvin Dean Watson." He stuck a calloused hand out to shake Slocum's.

"You doing all right today, Dana Ruth?" Slocum asked.

"Fit as fiddle. You must have walked a long ways."

Slocum laughed at her concern. "A real long ways."

"Well, get in here. I'll fry you some eggs and we've got bread and butter."

"Good, I'm starved nigh to death. You two seen anyone besides me the last two days?"

"Tell him what you told me, Dana Ruth," her brother said.

"Well, I seed a man on a buckskin horse on the ridge

north of here. First thought it was a damned Injun. They got buckskins."

"What day was that?" Slocum asked her.

"The day that ya was here."

"What did he look like?"

"He rode a buckskin horse and had a cowboy hat on. Come over here." She took him by the hand to the doorway and pointed. "See that space up there? Above the rock out-cropping? He was sitting on a yellow hoss up there."

"Light or dark hat?"

She dropped her shoulders in surrender. "I can't remember."

They went back to the table, and she served him eggs and biscuits and flour gravy. "Hope I got enough. Bet you ain't ate in hours."

"Been a while. You've never seen him, Calvin Dean?"

"No, sir, but I went up and looked. His horse is crooked-legged. His left hoof turns out and right hoof turns in. Not bad unless you look hard at them tracks."

"You must have learned tracking from a Comanche. He could almost tell you what a horse looked like seeing his tracks."

Calvin Dean beamed. "I studied lots of them tracks. Now who do you reckon it is that shot your horse?"

"One of three people. A pushy rancher named Yates. A mad killer named Chelsey Farnam. Or a man I don't know."

"This Farnam kill someone with you?"

"Yes. A woman I came to help. Yates framed her husband for horse stealing. She wrote and asked me to come help her. I did, and Farnam jumped us in the night, kicked the hell out of me, and kidnapped her. I found her grave a day ago up where Red was."

"Oh, mercy, that's terrible," Dana Ruth said, making a sad face.

"You sure it was her?" Calvin Dean asked.

Slocum nodded and swallowed hard. "I'm sure, I dug her up and replanted her."

Both of them gave shocked looks at each other.

Slocum stopped eating. "I had to know."

"My lands, Slocum," she began, looking at him concerned. "Wasn't that hard to do?"

"Hardest damn thing I ever did in my life—had a broken-handled shovel—"

"You could have come got us. We'd of helped you."

"I know, Calvin Dean. I know you two would have. It was something I had to do."

She agreed. "Things like that you have to do it yourself. Can't nobody do them fur ya."

"Right," he said to her. "I've got a good saddle up there in the big dry wash. A man named Plover made it in Dodge for me. Buzzards should lead you to my dead horse. If I don't come back by, you can have it. Otherwise, I'll give a ten-dollar reward. Now, I need a horse to ride out of here. You sell me one?"

"Hell, no," she said. "We'll loan you one, and you can bring him back here when you're done with him."

Slocum looked up at the canvas roof's underside. She just wanted company again. "That's a deal."

Calvin Dean rose to go after him. "I'll be getting him saddled."

"Wait, Calvin Dean. I can't take your saddle."

"It's a spare. I'll ride up and get yours today."

"I am obliged to both of you."

"I'm just proud to have a chance to meet you." Calvin Dean left to go saddle a horse for him. With her hand in the crook of his arm, Dana Ruth lead Slocum down to the pens.

He about smiled at her possessive ways. When he was ready to leave, he gave her a peck on the forehead, took the reins, swung up on the bay horse, and turned him around. "Let me warn you that either of those men are killers. Better watch yourselves, be very careful. And thanks for the horse here. I'll bring him back."

"You better," she said smugly. "Or I won't loan you another."

Calvin Dean laughed and shook his head. "You'll find she's a tough woman."

Slocum waved and rode off. At noon, sun time, he crossed the Verde, and saw two riders coming off the steep slope in a hard run. At the sight of him, they set their ponies down on their heels.

"It's him!" Johnny shouted.

"Where's his red horse?" Star asked his brother.

"Shot by a bushwhacker yesterday," Slocum said. "You fellas seen anyone new around riding a buckskin horse?"

"No. Is he Farnam?"

"No, he may be someone new." Slocum twisted in the saddle and pointed. "There's a ranch west of here. Later on, I'll need to send this horse back to the people who own him. You think you can find it, Star?"

The youth stared up the mountain. "Yeah, I can find it."

"Good folks. A brother and sister running their own ranch." He motioned for the brothers to ride east. "Her name's Dana Ruth, he's Calvin Dean. You ever met them?"

Star nodded matter-of-factly and then looked back at the mountain as if being certain he'd recognize where to go when the time came.

"Anything happened in Oxbow?" Slocum asked.

Johnny laughed. "Nothing happens in Oxbow unless you bring in a prisoner on a leash."

"Well, when we get up on the flatter ground, we're going to lope."

"What're you going to do next?" Star asked.

"Find out who this hired gun is."

"Can we help you?" Johnny asked.

"Some, if you keep your head down and don't get caught spying."

"There you go, Johnny. We're on his team." And the three loped away. Finding Amy's killer and putting Yates out of business were going to be two tough projects. Even with his main man gone, Yates could hire some worse ones. This buckskin-wearing stranger could be the one Slocum was looking for. He'd know in a day or so.

13

Hallie came to the lighted doorway, drying her hands on a flour-sack towel when they rode up. "Took you long enough to find him."

"Aw, Maw," Johnny said, stepping down. "We rode plumb to the Verde River before we found him."

She laughed. "There's ham and beans on. I'll make some coffee." She turned to Slocum, "You have trouble?"

"Here, go ahead and tell her," said Star. "We'll put the horses up." He rode in and took Slocum's reins.

"Tell me what?" She herded Slocum inside the house.

"Long story. I suspect Farnam murdered Amy. Someone did anyway. I can't think of anyone else that mean."

"You found her body?" Hallie folded her arms as if cold.

"He'd buried her. I found the grave—"

"You sure it was her?"

"Yes—positive. I had to be. I dug her up."

"Oh, no!" She ran over and hugged his head. "That must have been terrible."

"I had to know." Her fresh-smelling starched and ironed dress tickled his nose.

"Yes, yes. Oh, Slocum. Why are all these people so cruel?"

"I have no idea, Hallie."

She swallowed hard, released him, and went to finish filling her coffeepot. "Then what did you do?"

"I was looking for my horses that this rancher up there said were running loose north of him. Actually, that's where I found her grave, in the far north end of the basin. I'd started back here when someone shot my roan horse out from under me, and the rest of the horses ran off. Sure did lots of walking to borrow that one out there."

"I imagine you did. When Bollie and that bobtailed packhorse showed up here, those boys had to go look for you," she said.

"They found me."

"Farnam's the one that shot your horse?"

Slocum shook his head. "No. I think Farnam fled that country. Dana Ruth Watson had seen this man a few days ago scouting their place. He rides a buckskin horse."

"Those two Watson kids making it all right? I worry a lot about them. They sure act grown up, but running a cow outfit up there is no kid's job."

"They seem to be making it."

"I guess I wasn't much older than that when the boys' father and I married and headed up here to stake us out a place." She glanced up as the boys came in the doorway and hung their hats on pegs. "Wash up. The stew's hot."

Slocum nodded to her, so she'd know they could talk later. He went and joined the hand washers at the dry sink where she had water, soap, and towels laid out for them.

"Oh, Ma, we spotted two more one-oh-three-branded calves on our mamma cows going up there," Star said.

"Fresh branded?" Slocum asked.

"Yeah, fresh." Star looked angry. "I catch them Albert boys using a running iron on anyone's calves, I guarantee you that they won't need Sunday clothes anymore."

"Easy, easy there with that kinda talk," Hallie said, serving them steaming bowls of stew.

Star gave her a cutting look, then dropped his gaze to the food. "I better not catch them is all I can say."

"Anyone seen or heard from U.S. Marshal Sam Hendren?" Slocum asked, cutting into the conversation.

"I've heard he was still getting a bunch of folks to testify to the grand jury," Hallie said.

"I guess he's busy."

After supper, the boys went up to the bunkhouse, leaving Hallie and Slocum to sit at the fireplace and talk. The logs in the hearth, every once in a while, when the flames hit the sap, made small explosions and sparks flew out in the blazes.

"Where will you go after this is all over?" she asked.

"Down the road," he answered.

"You told me when you were recovering you had no roots."

He dropped forward so his elbows were on his knees. Watching the flames lick up the space above the red glowing logs, he nodded. "My past has molded my life for me. Some bounty hunter or Kansas deputy in a Prescott bar will hear someone say, 'Slocum? Oh, he was over at Oxbow last I heard.'"

"Such a shame. There's no one to run Amy's place. You could step right in."

Next thing he knew, she was standing in front of him, pulling him to his feet. "You know we have no one. So we can't hurt anyone doing what we want to do. Do you mind?"

He looked into her blue eyes. "Hell, no." Then he kissed her. In fact, he was right proud of her idea—might take his mind away from all the things that had been boring into it.

When he started to talk, she pressed her fingertips to his mouth. "No apology is necessary."

She went over, put some wood on the fire, and then returned to him. They kissed slowly, the friction of two flammable objects being rubbed together until flames began to spring up inside both of them. He paused, and began unbuttoning her dress down the front in the wavering orange glow of the fireplace. She shrugged it off her shoulders, smiled at him, and then laid it carefully over the back of a kitchen chair. Must be her best one, he decided, and took her back to kiss her again. His hand soon cupped the teacup-sized breast under the chemise, and she quickly drew the undergarment off over her head. Her slender form glowed in the firelight as he watched while he toed off his boots. She helped him undress, and then led him to the bed.

With a wink for her, he held up the covers, and they soon buried themselves in each other's arms. Her lithe body squirmed and molded itself against him, their mouths sipping honey from each other and the growing shaft between them becoming more and more obvious. She reached down and put him in her moist gates. Then her hips moved against him, and she cried out when he slipped past her ring of fire.

They hung on the edge of a cliff, suspended in midair, then floated into the clouds. Her hair swirled over her face and she combed it aside for his kisses. Lips parted, she moaned as the heat of their actions moved them higher and higher.

His world spun like a roulette wheel around him. Her hip bones were against him, hunching to his every effort to reach the depths of her body. Then he kissed her hard. Prepared for the charge, she clutched his upper arms and strained. The end blew off his skintight dick when he came.

He came with the fury of a cannon—then again.

Tightly embraced, they fell out of the sky into the hollowed-out mattress. He clung to her forever.

"I . . . needed that," she said, and kissed him. "More than I even knew."

At last, on his back with her sprawled half on top of him, they savored the moment, drained and satisfied. He looked up at the bottom side of the shingles in the dancing fireplace light. It had no doubt taken lots of their labor to build this cabin. Her husband must have been a real craftsman. Every rafter fit without a gap. It was a cabinetmaker's perfection.

Her face rested on Slocum's chest. His palms rubbed over her shoulders and back.

"When you're spoiled by the love of a man, you really miss it when he is no longer around to fulfill that need," she said. "I wondered if I ever could give that much of myself to another—you made that easy. Thanks, Slocum. Thanks."

Then she moved on top of him, reached under, and inserted his half-stiff dick inside her, and lowered herself down. "He must not be through with me."

He laughed and shook his head at her. "Not yet anyway."

Before dawn, he awoke to her stoking the stove. The candle lamp on the table lighted her activities. She straightened and closed the stove door. "Sleep well, sir?"

"The best, ma'am."

"When you go out, ring the triangle to wake the boys."

"That the all-clear signal?"

She shook her head over his remark and looked embarrassed. "Just ring it."

"I will. I was only teasing you."

She nodded. "I know, but it is uncomfortable—well, a little bit. Not that I didn't enjoy it—but, well, you want to set a good example for your boys."

With his pants on, he went over barefoot and hugged her. "I realize that. I am sure if they knew, they'd understand."

She kissed him. "Maybe."

"I need to do some scouting today. They wanted to help me."

Busy rolling out the biscuit dough to cut, she nodded again. "They need that experience, too. I will confine my worries about their safety to myself."

"I'm not stealing them."

"Go on. I know that. A mother simply has to worry so much."

Slocum emptied his bladder outside in the darkness. The temperature was low enough to cause frost on things. Then he rang the triangle until a lamplight shone in the bunkhouse window. They'd be coming.

"They must be up," he said, coming inside with an armload of wood.

"They usually are good about getting up. And with the notion they might get to go scouting, I imagine they slept light last night. Where will you go today?"

"I want to check out Yates and see if that buckskin horse is up there. If he's hired a gunman, he might be a loner."

"What does that mean?" She was busy loading the biscuits in the Dutch oven.

"There are back-shooters that keep to themselves. Maybe not trust anyone. This man could be one of them."

"How will you find out?"

"Just do some scouting."

Johnny came bursting in. "Morning."

"Good morning, Johnny," she said, putting the lid on the oven and placing red-hot coals on the lid as she situated it in the edge of the fireplace over more coals.

"Did Slocum tell you we were invited to do some scouting with him?" he asked his mother.

"He mentioned it."

"I just wanted to be sure you knew about it."

"What did she say?" Star asked, coming in the door.

"He told her."

"Is it all right?"

She laughed and then shook her head in amazement. "I guess the vote was three to one. But remember, these men are real killers."

"Oh, we know all about them. They shot Slocum's great horse," Johnny said, taking his place at the table,

"We saddled Bollie for you to ride. Figured that old Texas horse they loaned you might fall off a bluff," Star said to Slocum as he finished washing his hands.

"Thanks, fellas."

"You know since we lost Dad," she said hustling around with breakfast, "I've kinda run things. I've come to see this since you came along."

Slocum held his hands up. "Not guilty."

"Just so you know," she said.

"Where we going first?" Star asked.

"I'll want to stop by and talk to Tommy," said Slocum. "He may know about the shooter. Then we'll go look over the Yates place. I'm thinking more and more this fella is some kind of hired killer that stays out in the brush."

"That means he won't be easy to catch."

"Right, Johnny. And like a sidewinder, we won't know what bush he's under."

Hallie looked at the ceiling for help. "Sounds dangerous."

"Naw, Ma, we're just scouting."

"I know. Keep your head down anyway."

The three rode out and headed for Oxbow. Hallie sent along some dry cheese and biscuits to eat should they need to. Each one carried a blanket in case it turned cold or they were outside after sundown.

"Better go buy us some candy to suck on." Slocum gave Star the money, and told Johnny to watch their horses while he went inside the Irish Saloon.

He found the place empty, and Tommy came from the back. "What did you learn?" Tommy asked. "I was getting worried about you."

"Farnam killed Amy."

"Oh, dear God, how sad. You find him?"

Slocum shook his head, and looked around to be certain they were alone. "Has there been a stranger in here rides a buckskin horse?"

"Not that I can recall. What's he done?"

"Shot a good horse out from under me. I think he's a hired killer, too. A loner, you know what I mean?"

"The very worst kind there is. You're thinking he works for Yates?"

"I don't have lots of other enemies, I hope—in this country."

"No. Yates and his rannies have been making the rounds again. He's telling folks they need to clear out. Wouldn't surprise me if they don't lynch him."

"Lynching don't solve much."

"Maybe not, but folks are getting more upset. Them fresh

one-oh-three brands are still showing up and the brand inspector ain't come by yet."

"Send word by the telegram office to have the governor request he get up here and meet with me."

"I doubt it does much good." Tommy shook his head in defeat.

"We'll see."

"All right. You be careful out there."

"See you later." Slocum went outside and saw Johnny had dismounted.

"Star says them damned Albert brothers were in the store earlier and rode south."

Slocum looked around. "Where did Star go?"

"Ah-ah, to see Miss Abby. But he won't be long. He ain't got fifty cents."

"Fifty cents?"

"That's what them whores charge in the morning, ain't it?"

Slocum was taken back. "I didn't know Oxbow had any."

"Oh, yeah." Johnny bobbed his head. "They've got three. Abby, her mother, and another gal named Sweet Pea have a dugout up the wash. Star's kinda soft on Abby, but don't tell Ma. She'd sure skin us both."

"You ever been up there?"

"Just with him, and I held the horses while he went inside. Them other two are old women. They came out and kinda of embarrassed me about them giving me free lessons."

"He stay in there long?"

"Oh, he stays in there a long time if he's got fifty cents. Then he complains them other two say he's had enough and run him off."

"Reckon he has had enough?"

Red-faced, Johnny ducked his head. "Don't ask me. I don't know one thing about it 'cept what I hear."

"Here he comes," Slocum said.

"Don't tell him a thing I said."

"I won't."

"Learn anything?" Star asked, taking his reins and swinging in his saddle.

"Nothing. You learn anything?"

"I learned my gal's going to marry Kent Morris next Sunday."

"Who's he?" Slocum asked.

"He owns a small freight line," Johnny said.

"Sorry to hear about it. She still taking on clients?"

"How did you—I guess so. Why?"

"I've got five dollars. Maybe today you ought to go back and get all that you want before she quits."

Star narrowed his eyes in disbelief. "You serious?"

"Here's the money. Me and Johnny ain't telling a soul. We'll meet you at Bailey's corrals late this afternoon. We ain't there by sundown, you ride home and say we split up. One more thing. Be as careful as you can, listen for any word about the buckskin horse man. He may have been there, too."

Star shook his head. "Why are you doing this?"

"I've been in a deal like that and didn't have the money for another round. Always wished I'd had one more round with her."

Star pushed his hat back on his shoulders and went to laughing. "Slocum, I like you more and more."

They separated. Slocum and Johnny rode north. Slocum suspected they were on a lost mission, but he needed to see if this ambusher was at the Yates place.

He wanted some answers, but doubted he'd learn much up there. Still, they needed to check.

14

"No buckskin in the corral," Johnny said, lying beside him on the ground and using the telescope to study things at Yates's headquarters.

"We'll stay here for a while and watch things before we pull out."

"Fine with me. Where do you reckon them Albert brothers were going?"

"Amy's place. Where else could you brand calves and no one bother you?"

Johnny shook his head. "Them sonsabitches need a branding iron up their asses."

"They ever change who's working the law in Globe, they may face a long prison term."

"That might be like looking for an ice storm on July Fourth."

Slocum laughed. "It could happen."

"Could I ask you some questions?"

Slocum looked over at him. "Sure."

"I've been around stock all my life. I've seen horses breed mares, bulls do cows, boars sows, and even sheep doing it. Now tell me how humans do it."

"Best way is if she's willing."

"Willing? What does that mean?"

"In this Abby's case, she's trading money for her services. So you pay her and she's willing. Other girls expect you to marry them and then they give you services."

"Is it hard to learn how to do it?"

"No, it'll come to you pretty fast. Just go real easy the first time. Don't rush doing anything and while you're doing it, savor it. Now, you do it with an honest woman she might get pregnant. Then you have to do the right thing. Either haul her to a doctor or marry her."

"What'll the doctor do?"

"Clear out her system."

"I'm learning. Sorry I'm so dumb. But I knew I didn't want to start on them other two old women. No, sirree."

Amused by the boy's answer, Slocum began thinking about Soffie McCall. A girl from a farm near the Slocum farm in Georgia.

Soffie had freckles—all over. He found that out the day they snuck off and went to the river. She whispered about meeting him at Brown's Ford on Tuesday when he danced with her on Saturday night.

He thought she wanted to go fishing, so early that morning he beat on an iron bar stuck in the ground and drove up enough river worms to fill two rusty cans. Then he strapped on a big knife to cut some cane poles. Put several lines all ready with fishhooks, lead weights, and corks in his saddle-bags. As well as two stringers made up to hang the fish on. He was thinking Soffie was going to be all right. Imagine her inviting him to go fishing with her. Most girls would have turned their nose up at that sort of thing. And he didn't mind that she wanted it secret. No telling why. Far as anyone at his house knew, he was going fishing by himself.

He met her at the ford, and she had a black boy named Seth to tend her horse and the one he rode. She came running over dressed in a fancy blue skirt, black knee boots, a frilly blouse, and a vest. They didn't look much like fishing clothes. And the silly flat hat she had to hold on to as she ran. The hat wasn't sensible for fishing in either.

"Oh, you really came." She glanced back toward the horses grazing in the meadow. "I have a picnic lunch and a blanket. We can go somewhere where we're alone, can't we?"

"Sure, there's places in the cane around the bend."

"Good. We'll get my things and go then."

"I'll get my fishing lines—"

She caught his arm and stopped him. "We can do that later."

"Sure—" What did she want to do? His knees began to feel real weak. Was she—

"Seth, come get Master Slocum's horse and bring my picnic basket and blanket over here."

The black boy came on the double, bowed to Slocum, and set the basket and blanket down. "I's hobble him, sah?"

"That will be fine. Thank you, Seth."

"You sure be welcome."

"You don't have to tell a slave thank you," she said, irritated. "You'd be busy all day if you do that."

She gave the blanket and the basket to Slocum; then they set out for the river's bend. She whirled around in the wildflowers like a ballerina, caught a black butterfly, and then released him to fly away. Her reddish brown hair glistened in the patches of sunlight coming through the sycamores and walnut. She waved the silly hat in her hand at things unseen, and smiled big back at him because he was lagging behind. The weight of the blanket and heavy basket was telling on him. She finally led the way down through the tall bamboo and found them a glen. Sunlight shone on the rippling river water.

"What a glorious place. Spread the blanket out so we may sit upon it. Could you write poetry here?"

He swallowed hard. "Yes, I guess, if I knew how."

"Oh, you start easy. Roses are red, violets are blue. And I am happy to be here. Just me and you. There, how was that?"

"Good. I'm not into poetry and rhyme, I guess."

He dropped to his knees, and she crawled over to put her head in his lap. That shocked him. Her reddish curls spilled out and her knees, clad in snow white stockings, were sticking out exposed.

"In these words of mine . . ."

"I seldom find the time."

"Oh, that is good," she said, praising him, then crossed her legs so one was kicking up and down like a pendulum. "To take—no—no. If I kissed you, would you tell?"

"Not if you meant it and it went well."

"Oh." She scrambled up and sat astradle his lap. "Always close your eyes when you kiss a girl. It makes her feel that you are more sincere."

"All right."

They kissed. In the process he about fell over, except he reached over her to catch himself and discovered she wore no underwear. In his hand was the smooth skin of her butt, and a bolt of lightning struck him warning he was on dangerous ground.

"This outfit is too confining," she said. "Poets must be free."

Swallowing became hard for him as she went to unbuttoning the front of her blouse.

"You may help me."

"Ah—sure."

So with shaky hands, he undid some buttons, but she was ten times faster than his stiff fingers. Quickly, she peeled the heavy starched garment open to expose a chemise of silk. Her small breasts pointed out like tents. Struggling to her feet, she rose and hung it on a limber bamboo pole. Then she pranced around him, repeated a line of poetry again and again, making him dizzy following her. At last, she dropped to her knees in front of him and cupped his face in her small hands to kiss him.

"Oh, Slocum, I am so excited about this day of creativity."

He was running his hand up and down the backs of her

legs over the socks and then the flesh of her firm ass. His heart was pounding, and she kissed him again, this time with more tongue than lips.

"Let's lie down side by side."

He was willing. "Sure."

She looked over at him. "You must be careful. I am a virgin."

"Oh, I will."

She smiled at his reply and he leaned over and kissed her, rubbing the top of her leg and inching the chemise higher. Soon he found his hand was in the stiff pubic hair, and she raised her leg and gave him access to her seam. Close to peeing in his pants, he discovered her moist vagina with his middle finger, and she opened her legs even more for his entry.

This was the fountain of a woman. He'd spied on slaves having sex in the hay or up against a tree. The more he probed in her, the harder she breathed. Soon, he was as deep as he could go. She pulled him down on top of her. They were wet-kissing, and she sounded like a freight train breathing so hard.

"Get your pants down—oh—hurry," she said in a loud whisper.

In seconds, his pants were down, and he discovered his dick was hard like it was many mornings when he first woke up. The only thing that relieved it was jacking off.

On top of her, he felt red-faced for being so stiff and still half dressed.

"Oh, put it in me." She held her forehead like someone who'd eaten too much ice.

Obeying her instructions, he raised up, took his rock-hard dick, and stuck it in the pink lips of her pussy. Over her, he gave it a hunch with his aching ass, and she gave a cry like he'd hurt her, and then she threw her arms around him.

"Give it all to me."

She meant she wanted all his dick inside her. Oh, well, what the hell. So he gave it to her. His world became a wild dizzy ride with his brain centered on his dick pumping in and out of her. Bracing himself so he didn't crush her, he tried to compare screwing her to everything he loved to do—like play baseball, bet on racehorses, climb tall trees, win a stake race himself. Nothing compared. Nothing he could think of even resembled the excitement of this urgent drive to send her flying, he guessed.

Then a hard cramp struck his right leg—oh God, why now? Then a new feeling gathered in his scrotum, and he came in one long hard drive up and out of his skintight dick. He rolled off her, getting up, tangled his ankles in his pants, falling on his face trying to escape the frozen muscle in his leg.

"You all right?" she asked.

"I have a cramp in my leg that's killing me." Seated on his butt, he tried to work it out until finally it relaxed. And with sweat running down his face, he tried to recall every second of the time he'd spent poking her.

She came over on her knees and began to hug his head, then kissed him. "That was wonderful. How can I ever repay you?"

Do it again? He better not ask for that. She might think he was sex-crazy. Like that old dog they had that tried to screw everything that would stand still for him. They'd caught him screwing a sheep in a pen once, and Slocum had wondered what a dog-sheep cross would look like. It never took because all the lambs the following February were normal-looking.

"Would you like to see all of me?"

"Yes, ma'am."

"Since we are now bonded, I don't think it would hurt. Take off your clothes, too."

What did she mean bonded? Hell, he wanted to see her tits anyway. So he unwrapped his legs, pulled his boots off and then shed his shirt, watching her all the time gather the chemise and raise it up higher and higher until her breasts were exposed. They were small white tents with huge knot-like pointed pink nipples. But the sight of them made the saliva flow in his mouth. He gathered her to him, bent over, and suckled on the right one.

Sucking on her teat was to him like stealing a neighbor's watermelons. You sure felt guilty doing it, but man, oh, man, she sure tasted wonderful. But doing that caused another problem. He was building another hard-on and fast.

"Oh, Slocum," she moaned. "I can see we must do it again."

He raised up with the smell of her perfume in his nose and the lavender flavor in his mouth. Without further discussion, he climbed on top of her and put his sore dick back to work inside her. That went on for hours. Until, finally holding her obviously sore crotch with both hands, she shook her head at him.

"I love you doing that to me, but I am on fire down there. Oh, I must go home and find some salve. But I love you for making this such a special day."

He rose and they kissed. They'd never again sneak small kisses. It was hungry mouths, saliva and hot tongues. For the final time, he squeezed and played with her teats.

Carefully, he helped her dress. She stopped and began to shake her head. "And we never ate a thing. Oh, well. Seth can eat all of it on the way home. He's always hungry."

She laughed freely.

That was Slocum's first and last time to make love to Soffie. She became engaged six weeks later to a rich older man that owned a sea house and a large plantation.

She sent him a note.

Dear Slocum,

I fear our love was so great that day that we caused a baby to be awakened in my belly. Don't worry about me. Carlson Humphrey needs an heir and has never had one with three wives. I will be his fourth, but I have what he needs, so you did us a big favor. Come see me on the Gulf or at our plantation. I am certain he'll want more.

Love,
Soffie

"Slocum," Johnny said in a low voice, bringing him out of his daydreaming. "Yates is riding out. By himself."

Slocum took the scope and saw the old man head up the canyon on a bay horse. That wasn't the way to town.

"Where's he going?"

"I don't know, Johnny, but we're going to find out. Let him go a ways and we can get our horses. He may be going to meet that bushwhacker."

"Good. I was getting bored."

"Spying is boring business, but sometimes you learn things."

"Yes. I know. Guess we'll have to tell Star all about it. Him off saying good-bye to Miss Abby."

Slocum about laughed out loud. Star was having his "Soffie Day," and Johnny would have one of his own sometime. Lord, that sun felt good.

15

"Holy cow. There's a man sitting a yellow horse coming off that mountain," Johnny said, peering through the brass scope.

"That's our man." Slocum sat cross-legged on the ground. He took the telescope and studied the rider. Just what he thought—a loner. Meeting Yates up there in the hills. Where was this man's camp? They'd need to find it.

"What do you figure about him?"

"Where up here is a good place to camp?"

"There's an old miner's shack over on Dead Cow Wash. It's about three-four miles from over there," Johnny said. "It ain't much, but there is a good spring there."

"How far from the ranch?"

"Maybe ten miles, maybe less."

"We need to pay him a surprise visit."

Johnny nodded his head, looking thoughtful. "I'm sure pleased you brought me along. I've learned a lot about these kinda deals."

"I hope you don't ever need to use it. Let's go. We don't want to tip our hand."

Johnny checked the sun time. "We may catch Star going back."

"I thought so, too. Go easy on him. He's had a bad day."

"I don't know how. We've done all the work." Then he shook his head, embarrassed. "And he got all the pussy."

They both laughed, and rode off to the south.

Star was waiting for them at Bailey's pens.

"You fellas learn anything?" he asked, looking them over.

"We have an idea where that ambusher is staying at," Johnny said.

"Good. We going after him?"

"In time," Slocum said as he watched the youth pile into his saddle with a one-handed bound off the ground.

"Oh, I only spent two dollars of your money." He booted his horse over toward Slocum. "Didn't help a thing. She's still going to marry that peckerwood—Sunday."

"Why, you can make three more stops there before Sunday."

"Naw, she kinda asked me not to do that."

"Guess you got her out of your system?"

"No, not out of my system. I'll always remember her. But I kinda understand what she's doing now. Being a lady of the night ain't all that great, and she's got a chance to quit it. I have nothing to offer her. Hell, I'm a momma's boy who lives at home."

"And that ain't so bad either. Your mom needs you two, and you both will have ranches of your own some day."

"Slocum—" Star let out a deep breath. "I want to thank you for sending me back. All I could think about was myself and what I was losing. Hell, she had a lot bigger problems than I had. And I've got to admit that that peckerwood is brave, too—marrying her and all."

"Keep the three bucks and buy me and Johnny some more candy tomorrow. We about ate it all today."

"Slocum, you know it's been a real big day for me, and Star, too. You ever think about ranching around here?" He looked hard at Slocum for an answer.

"Boys, I've left some things undone over my right shoulder. There's a reward on me. And a couple of Kansas deputies stay after me. Actually, as much as I like the land and the good people and I'd love to stay here, it wouldn't work."

"Ma could sure use you," Star said. "I can tell you and her get along."

"Thank goodness she has the two of you."

"Well, we appreciate all you're doing for us."

"Let's ride, boys. She's holding supper for us."

At their ranch, Hallie came to the lighted door to greet them. She had a wide smile on her face as she spoke to them. "I was about to wondering where you three galoots were at."

"I'll put your horse up," Johnny said and led him off with Star as Slocum went toward the house.

"Thanks," Slocum said, then turned back to Hallie. "We did some good today. I think we located that ambusher. Saw him and Yates meet."

"Good. Those boys of mine really like you."

"They're good boys. You're lucky."

"Come in and wash up. Yes, I am lucky. I count my blessings every day. Strange enough, I even count you as a big one."

He hugged her and kissed her. "Me, too."

Then he washed up, and the boys soon came in from the corral.

After supper, she played the fiddle. "When Johnny Comes Marching Home," "Turkey in the Straw," "John, John, the Gray Goose is Gone," and finished with "Virginia Waltz."

The boys went off to the bunkhouse.

She stoked the fireplace and turned back to look at Slocum. "I'd swear that Star smelled like perfume tonight."

He walked over and hugged her. "I want you to promise me you won't ever tell a soul what I am going to tell you."

She wet her lip and looked up at him. "I promise. I hope I'm strong enough to hear this."

He rocked her in his arms. "You are." And he told her about her eldest son's day. When he finished, she sniffled.

"Oh, my. How generous of you. I would not have had that answer for him. I'd've fallen to pieces, I think."

"We all make some bad moves in our lives. That girl wasn't a bad move. She just didn't fit. But he needed to go back and learn why. He was as honest as a man can be in such a situation."

"Oh, Slocum, it's hard to be a mother at times. They need their dad. Though I don't know if he'd've been that understanding."

"Hallie, you're doing a fine job. It was something that he just couldn't come and discuss with you."

"What if I blow out the lamp?"

"Do that girl. I'm with you." He playfully clapped her on the ass when she started off toward the lamp.

"If I told you how many times I thought about you today, you'd think I was silly."

"You know, I could say the same thing to you." He toed off his other boot.

In the bed at last, her sleek body molded to his, they kissed with unsuppressed need for each other, slowly drowning in a whirlpool of want and the need to be one. Deep into their session, his back and hips ached as they climbed a mountain. He came hard, and they floated down into the bed, clinging to each other, and slept.

Her efforts to make breakfast awoke him. She delivered him a cup of steaming coffee. "You talked a lot in your sleep last night."

"I say anything to scare you?"

"No. You keep saying, 'No, Bradley. No.'"

"He was a young West Pointer out of Camp Steward who was convinced he could wipe out a band of Cheyenne with his small company of men."

"Did you convince him?"

"I thought I did, but while I was away looking for some horse thieves, he went against what he promised me. They drew him into a pursuit, and he met a much larger force over the next rise that left half his men either dead of wounded."

"It's a wonder you sleep at all."

"When I get to a safe place like yours, I really sleep."

She came over and kissed him. "Good. I'm glad that you aren't afraid in my house."

He rose and hugged her. "We'll get this land cleared of the worst ones and it'll be a good place to live and ranch."

"You will always have a place here. You know that?"

"I told the boys yesterday why I couldn't stay forever."

"I know, but you could blow in here like a dust storm every once in a while. Get a fresh horse, a good night's sleep, and some sourdough biscuits if I don't burn these. Go ring the triangle." She rushed off to rescue her biscuits.

He went outside and rang the triangle. No worry. Those biscuits would be wonderful to eat. He looked to the west in the starlight. Silhouetted against the sky was the range of mountains that he had to cross to look for Farnam. He'd get that worthless bastard and tack his hide on the shithouse door.

He'd do it for Amy. Damn Farnam's bloody soul to hell . . . .

16

Leaning back in a captain's chair with his dusty boots bracing himself on the back two legs, U.S. Marshal Sam Hendren sat whittling on a cedar stick on the saloon's front porch.

"I been wondering if you were coming to town," the man said, smoothing his large mustache. He snapped the knife shut, set the chair down, and rose.

"What've you got for me?" Slocum asked.

"How about a deputy's badge? Governor has appointed me acting sheriff of Gila County until an election can be held to replace Sheriff Cummings, who is charged with several things—embezzlement of county funds, failure to fulfill his job about the cattle thieves you brought in, failure to investigate a rape, turning loose a convicted felon. The list goes on. Where is Mrs. Branch?"

"Buried over in Bloody Basin. Chelsey Farnam kidnapped her and then murdered her over there."

"Oh, damn. That is sad news. I thought they had arrested him."

"No. Her death points to him."

"I want you to help me arrest those rustlers you talked

129

about." He turned to the Greenwood brothers. "Who are these young men?"

"The rest of your posse. Star and Johnny Greenwood."

"Slocum says you're deputies, here's a badge." He fished out what had once been ten-centavo pieces as badges for each of them.

They thanked him with beaming pride.

"Now, I guess we'll arrest those cattle rustlers first. Oh, they have hired a new brand inspector. He should be here in two days. The other one was in on that false arrest of your old friend Ernie Branch. I hated to hear Branch was killed. And worse, his wife—you've had hell up here and no help from the local law."

"I bet we can find the Albert brothers marking calves down on her place. Right, Slocum?" Star said.

"Yes, I imagine that's the easy pickings."

"I'll get my horse and we'll round them up," said Hendren. "Slocum, tell me what else I need to know. We have a warrant for Yates. It's for night riding and harassing his neighbors. Not as strong a charge as I wanted. But Cummings has a deputy named Scroggins that I think will turn state's evidence. He's scared as hell."

"That could be the answer right there," Slocum said.

Hendren agreed.

When they reached Amy's range later that morning, they used Hendren's field glasses and Slocum's telescope looking for the thread of smoke from a branding fire.

"We may have to get higher," Slocum said, and they set out for a place up the slope.

Slocum noticed buzzards. They were really turkey vultures circling in the sky, but folks called them lots of things. "Something is dead up there. Should we go look?"

"We better," Hendren said.

When they reached the file of cottonwoods on side of the sandy wash, he saw what had the birds of carrion so interested. Two bodies hung by their necks swinging on their ropes. The large blackbirds rose in flight at their approach. It was the Albert brothers—not a pretty sight.

Slocum rode in and cut them both down to fall in the sand. He dismounted, and felt the cold ashes where their running irons had been heated. It had been twenty-four hours since they had been alive, by his guess.

"Boys, go find their horses. I don't know her, but their mother will want them to have a funeral."

Star nodded. "We'll go look, Slocum." He took Johnny with him.

"You know, when you can't trust the law to do a decent job, then God-fearing folks take things into their own hands," Hendren said with a weary shake of his head.

"It's a bad situation. We've got laws in this land. Laws run higher than Cummings and his machine."

"Amen," Hendren said. "But it's been hard for folks to tell that up here. We better wrap them in blankets if you're dead set to take them home."

Slocum agreed. "Their mother—it would upset her worse if we shallow graved 'em."

"I expect you're right. Those boys already found their horses. They're bringing them back. How did you hook up with them?"

"Their mother tended to me after Farnam beat me up so bad."

"Guess it did take me forever to get up here. We can load these two now and get them home. Saved the government some money. You know about this fella who they were branding for?"

"I was going to ask you the same thing. His name is Drithers," Slocum said. "He's a cattle buyer, they said."

"We'll run him down, too," Hendren promised. The two of them loaded the older brother's wrapped body over the saddle first, and tied him down while Star held the reins. Next they strapped on the younger one.

Slocum noticed both Greenwood boys looked a little

taken aback by the lynching. It was no doubt their first experience dealing with one. Tough business. Like lots of things, hangings were easier to talk about than to actually deal with.

Finally, they turned off the Tonto Basin Road onto a set of long dry ruts that wound downhill toward an outfit. The kind of steep hill a horse like Bollie shifted his weight from side to side to descend. There were clothes blowing on a line. A woman taking her dry wash down turned and looked up at the riders and the bodies. Even at the distance, Slocum saw the shocked look in her eyes.

"Samuel!" she screamed, and carrying her dress, ran for the house. "Samuel!"

A man came out on the porch, a hard-faced man that searched their faces. The woman clung to the door frame muttering, "Oh, dear God, don't let it be my boys."

"Mr. Albert? I'm the temporary sheriff for Gila County. We were checking cattle this morning and discovered your sons hanging in a cottonwood—"

"Oh, no!" She screamed as she sunk to her knees. The cry hurt Slocum's ears.

"Who lynched 'em?" Samuel Albert demanded.

"We don't know," Hendren said. "We are only the messengers returning their bodies to you."

"Who hung them? Why did you do that?" He rushed out and tore the reins of the Albert brothers' horses from Star's hands.

"Mr. Albert, in case you didn't know, your boys were branding other folks' calves with a running iron."

"Not my boys." He hit his chest with his fist. "My boys weren't rustlers. Not my boys—you four hung 'em and then you turned them in like they were dead dogs."

"Samuel! Samuel!" she cried. "They're dead! My boys are dead!"

"Shut up, woman. I'll handle this."

"No! No! They're dead, Samuel."

"Gawdamnit, woman, shut up."

"They worked for a man named Drithers with a one-oh-three brand," Hendren said, looking at Slocum for reassurance. Slocum nodded.

"I don't know any Drithers and neither did my sons."

She began pulling on his arms and screaming at him. "Samuel, they're dead! Do you hear me?"

"Shut up, woman." He shoved her down in the dirt, then quickly picked up the reins of both horses again. "I'll see all four of you bastards in hell. You hear me!"

"Mr. Albert, we're sorry," Slocum said as they started to turn and leave. "Sorry we cut them down and tried to do the Christian thing for you."

"Christian?" Albert roared. "You're the devil's handymen. All of you. I'll get even. I'll get even with all of you for this even if it takes the rest of my life."

"Come on, boys, I've heard enough," Slocum said. "He shoves her down one more time while I'm here, I'll bust his head open."

The four started back uphill. Slocum could hear the woman's frantic screams, and looked back to see that Albert was slapping her around. Hendren put his hand on Slocum's arm to stop him. "I know what you're thinking right now. But he'll do worse to her when you're through with him and after you leave."

"Hard to swallow, though."

"He's crazy. We were only trying to help him," Johnny said.

Hendren agreed. "Folks get cornered, they do crazy things. I've seen it many time before. He's not ever going to believe anyone that tells him that they were rustling. He'll always say they hung two innocent boys."

"There's lots to being a deputy, ain't there?" Johnny asked.

"There's lots to learn," Hendren said.

Slocum surveyed the red western sky, then turned to the brothers. "It'll be after dark when we get back to your mom's. We better hustle. You want to join us?" he asked Hendren.

"Naw, but I'd like to go look for Farnam and this ambusher you've talked about."

"Whatever. They both need to be arrested. Hang some offense on them."

"I'm certain we can do that," Hendren said. "Want to meet me in the morning in Oxbow?"

"Sure, we'll be there," Slocum said, and the boys agreed.

"We've got a warm bunkhouse," Star said. "Ma does some great cooking."

"Thanks. I bet she does. I'll see you three then."

After they parted, Star led his brother and Slocum on a shortcut to their place. It was rougher country, but the trouble paid off as the last of twilight faded and they came over the final ridge and could see the light on in the house.

"Been one helluva day," Johnny said as they spread out on the flatter ground and headed in.

"I won't forget it," Star said. "I just can't believe how bad that man treated his wife."

"It stuck in my craw, too, but Hendren was right. If I'd broken it up, he'd've punished her for that later, too."

"I seen a few men when I've been in town do what I though was mistreat their wives over nothing, but that today really made me real upset," Johnny said.

"You boys been raised right. That's what it is."

"You never knew our paw, but we seen him, didn't we, Star? We seen him take a whip away from a man who was beating an overloaded team and use it on him."

"I felt sorry for the man before he got through with him. Then he made us tie our lariats on his wagon tongue and pull his rig up the bank."

Slocum dropped heavily out of the saddle at the yard gate. He undid his chaps and hung them on the horn.

"How are my men tonight?" Hallie stood on the porch, drying her hands on her apron. "Food's still hot. You two don't mess too long with those horses. Slocum can tell me part of the day's story while you do that. Bet it was different."

"It was, Mom," Star said.

Slocum nodded in agreement walking toward her—for her sons, it had been real different.

The two led the horses for the pens. Slocum paused at the stoop, nodded at her. When he stepped up, he squeezed her shoulder and then herded her inside the cabin. "It's been a helluva day."

After supper, when the boys were gone to the bunkhouse and they were in bed together, she asked him, "What did the boys think up there, do you reckon?"

"Afterward, they told me about their paw whipping a man who was beating his weak team and then pulling him out."

She rolled over on her back, then pulled the flannel sheet and feather quilt up to her chin. "I remember that. He made a good impression on those boys, didn't he?"

"Yes, he really did."

Then she rolled over toward him, raised up, dragged a small breast over his chest, and kissed him. "I know we're on borrowed time, but this bed's sure going to be empty when you have to leave it."

"It'll leave an empty spot for me, too."

"Guess since you've rode all day that you're real tired?"

He swung her over and climbed on top of her. "Not that tired, gal. Not that tired."

She laughed, raising her knees around him. "Good."

In the morning, he woke up when she did, and when the water was heated, he took a quick sponge bath, then used her late husband's razor and shaving brush to shave.

She found Slocum a shirt and britches she thought would fit and laid them out. "I'll wash yours today."

"Service is great around here," he said, giving her a kiss on the cheek as she worked to fry hashed potatoes.

"Good. Where are you and the posse going today?"

"I'll leave that to Hendren. I think he has a warrant for Yates. He wants that sharpshooter and Farnam."

"You think Farnam is still in the country?"

He shook his head. "Naw, but he's somewhere. Time to wake up the rest of the crew?"

She put down the turner and slipped her arms around him. Pressed up against him, he kissed her, and they savored each other until she broke her mouth away to say, "Just be careful."

"We will."

"Go wake your crew." He went outside and rang the triangle. Predawn's dim light shrouded the yard and grounds. When he turned, a bullet smashed into the cabin's log wall and the whine of rifle shot cracked the air. He dove headfirst inside the cabin's open doorway.

"Get back from the door," he shouted at her, scrambling for his rifle. The Winchester in his hands, he yelled to the boys. "Boys, stay inside. He's up on the south side somewhere."

"Where are you going?" she asked as he opened the back window and prepared to climb outside.

"Stay away from those front windows and doors. I'm going to try to outmaneuver him." His leg up on the sill, he slipped outside and dropped to the ground with the rifle.

"Is it the shooter?" Star shouted from the bunkhouse.

"Yeah, keep your heads down." He was past the house and headed for a clump of junipers he knew would block the ambusher's sight. But he had to get across the open ground in between, and another bullet to the right of him kicked up lots of dust.

"Slocum?" Star called out to him.

"I'm fine," he said from the pungent clump of evergreens. He needed to cut lots of distance down to ever use his own gun. That rifle the shooter was using was long-range and powerfully accurate, but the man had gotten tired of waiting. Another thirty minutes of light and hed've knocked Slocum off his horse. Slocum worked his way to the edge of the dense limbs, then crossed the open ground covered by another grove. With another move, he'd be in range.

He heard a horse snort, and realized from the sounds that

the sumbitch was fixing to ride off. He hit the open area on a run, and could see horse and rider swinging around. Stopping, he took aim and levered six fast shots after the man. But the distance was too great. Not enough rifle power either. The buckskin horse and rider cat-hopped up the mountain and disappeared in the brush.

Star, with his own rifle, joined him. "We need to get our horses?"

Slocum shook his head. "That would be asking to get shot. Never chase a fella like that. He has all the advantages and can simply sit down somewhere and shoot you. No, you need to wait till you can surprise him."

"That makes sense. How did he miss you?"

"Not enough light. Those telescopes don't work their best in less than full daylight."

"Makes sense. We still going to join Hendren?"

"Yes. I hope that the shooter worries all day that we're on his trail. Make him jumpy as a cat in a room full of rockers." Slocum clapped Star on the shoulder. "We better eat something. It's going to be a long day."

"He get close to you?" Johnny asked.

"Anytime someone is shooting at me, it's too close."

"I guess that's right."

Hallie came outside on the porch and looked at the mountain. "He's gone?"

"Long gone for now. He won't be back right away. When he thinks we've forgotten him, he'll come back if we haven't gotten him by then."

She hugged her arms against the coolness. "I'll pray that you have."

Hallie and the boys went inside. Slocum followed them after he made one more check of the mountain. Nothing in sight. He needed that shooter eliminated for certain.

17

Hendren waited on the saloon porch in a chair borrowed from inside. Not bothering to rise, he shoved his hat back on his head. "You boys sleep good last night?"

"We sure did," Johnny said. "Except Yates's bushwhacker got us all up trying to kill Slocum."

Hendren frowned at Slocum. "He get close?"

"Enough that I knew who he meant to shoot."

"He must have got away?"

"He did, but we decided not to pursue him or ride into one of his traps. Not tracking him could upset him more than trying to run him down."

"It could. That leaves us to arrest Yates and deliver him to Globe."

Slocum had a notion. "Star, we may be riding out of the country. I want you to go back to the ranch and stay with your mother. Be on your toes. He could come back there. Don't you take any chances."

A pained look of disappointment crossed Star's face. "Am I going to miss all the damn excitement?"

"You may have some of your own. He's a knowledgeable back-shooter. You remember that, and don't forget it."

"I'll handle it. I know we don't want anything to happen to Mom. You three be careful."

"That's a damn good idea," Hendren said, and scrubbed the side of his face with his palm. "Damn whiskers itch."

"I shaved mine off this morning," Slocum said, and laughed.

"I may do the same if I get the chance."

They parted with Star, who headed back for the ranch. Hendren went for the marshal's horse, while Johnny put his chair back inside, and when the lawman returned, they took the Tonto Basin Road north. Mid-morning, they came under the crossbar over the gate with the Bar O brand on it, and rode on for the Yates ranch headquarters. They had to cross the open grassland to the base of the juniper-covered hills. It was Slocum's first time to see the ranch from this direction. He knew the layout from above but it didn't feel quite right. There was something out of place, and he couldn't figure out what it was.

He turned the boy. "Johnny, keep your eyes and ears open. We could run into anything up here."

"Yes, sir. I understand. "

"Stay wide of me and the marshal. That way, we won't shoot each other."

"Yes, sir."

They reined up in front of the house. No saddled horses in sight. At long last, a short Oriental came to the doorway.

"No one home here. They all ride away early dis morning." The Chinaman made a shooing sign with his hands.

"Where were they going?"

"No tell me."

"But you know," Hendren said, dismounting and heading for the porch. "You boys look around. I'm looking inside."

"Who you?"

"The United States marshal. Where's your passport?"

"Oh, big mistake. Me American."

"I don't know if I believe that," Hendren said to the cook as Slocum sent Johnny to the left and he went right. There were no horses in the pens. He checked out the large half-open barn, and found the tack had been ransacked like someone had been looking for the best in there to take. Several old saddle hulls and broken headstalls lay strewn around.

Slocum came outside as Johnny cautiously opened the bunkhouse door nearby. The youth gave Slocum a nod and went inside, while Slocum checked other things in the wagon shed. Johnny soon reappeared.

"They left. I can tell. There ain't one picture of a naked woman left in there."

"Must be proof that they're gone." Slocum laughed.

"The safe's been cleaned out in the house," Hendren said, leaning out the window. "Yates got the word and ran on us."

"What's your Oriental friend saying?"

"He said that they left this morning riding north. Yates paid off all the hands and told them to ride clear of Oxbow."

"Who's with him?" Slocum asked as he headed in the direction of the house.

Hendren was gone from the window for a minute, and soon came back. "Charlie in here says two gunhands went with him. One was called Morris and the other Conroe."

"I've never heard of them," Slocum said.

Johnny shook his head. "I don't know those two either."

"Probably new hands he'd just hired," Slocum said. "We ran off the rest. Ask him about the man with the buckskin horse. He's been here. I saw him here, in fact."

Hendren turned back. "Who in the hell is the one rides the buckskin that was around here?"

"His name is Po-tis."

Slocum stopped. "Ask him if his name is Prentice."

"You know a Prentice?" Hendren asked over his shoulder, then turned back to Slocum. "He says that's his name. You know him?"

Slocum nodded. "The one I knew is a mean sumbitch."

"Could be him. You want to go after Yates? I can make

you two U. S. deputy marshals so that county lines won't bother you."

"Johnny, what do you think?" Slocum asked the youth.

"I'll go with you."

"Okay, we'll go after him."

"Good," Hendren said.

Slocum helped himself to some food from Yates's pantry. He also found Johnny a thick wool coat that would fit him. Going in the high country, they'd sure need more clothing. He made himself a poncho out of a heavy woolen blanket by cutting a hole in the center.

"You need to get word to Hallie and Star where we've gone. I hope to bring Yates back alive to stand trial."

"I'll get them word," Hendren promised. "Good luck. I know you're doing all this for Mrs. Branch—damn, I hate he killed her. That worthless sumbitch Farnam should have been cut when he was born."

"Or hit in the head."

"That would have saved us all lots of misery. You two be careful. Wire me in Globe when you can."

When the food was loaded in tow sacks and tied on their saddle horns, they headed north. Slocum wanted to make the high country by nightfall.

In a few hours, Johnny pointed out the snow on the mountains ahead. The short winter day soon began to wane. The bloody sunset blazed on the snow cover at that elevation they were in, though the road was still clear. Most of the white stuff was in the shade.

After dark, they reached Barnabus Ranch, and the old man who ran a saloon-store greeted them from the doorway. "You fellows out late, ain't 'cha?"

Vapors poured out of Slocum's mouth when he laughed. "Barnabus, what in the hell are you doing?"

"Taking care of trade. That you, Slocum?"

"Ain't Saint Nick. Me and this boy are starved."

"Aw, the woman, she's got plenty of food. Get in here."

Barnabus stepped out, and told Johnny where to put their horses and to feed them grain.

Slocum stopped at the doorway to shake his hand. "Yates ride by here today?"

"You looking for him?"

He nodded.

"Yeah, never stopped to say a word, but they watered their horses. There were two hard cases riding with him."

"Hired guns. His time ran out. Sheriff Cummings and some more of his bunch are in jail. Their deal to send Ernie Branch up on phony charges came back to haunt 'em."

"Good. How's Mrs. Branch?"

"Dead."

"Oh, bless her heart. What happened to her?"

"The man who Yates hired to rape and scare her off came back again. He left me for dead, then kidnapped her. Later, he murdered her over in Bloody Basin."

"The law looking for him?"

"They were supposed to have him in jail."

The old man shook his bushy face. "Woman, look, your favorite hombre is here."

"Slocum!" the thick-set Mexican woman in her thirties shouted, and rushed over to hug him. "I am so glad you stopped by, *mi amigo*."

Johnny came in quietly, shook Barnabus's hand, and nodded to the woman.

"Me, too," said Slocum. "Your fireplace feels great. Johnny Greenwood, this is Juanita Barnabus."

"I am so glad to meet you," she said to the youth.

"Me, too, ma'am."

"Get us some whiskey," Barnabus said to her, and turned back to Slocum. "You two hombres can eat and I can drink. As I told you, Yates and the others just watered their horses and rode on today. What else bad has happened?"

Juanita delivered both Johnny and Slocum big bowls of steaming beef stew and a stack of flour tortillas. With a grin when Slocum thanked her, she was off again.

He turned back to his friend. "The Albert brothers were hung."

"You know who did it?"

"Vigilantes. I don't really care. We caught the brothers red-handed branding a calf of Mrs. Branch. Amy and I arrested those two, took 'em to Globe, and Sheriff Cummings said they were too young. It would ruin their life to charge them, he said. Turned them loose."

"He did that?"

Juanita brought the bottle of whiskey with two glasses and set them down.

Slocum told her, "*Gracias*," because his friend had no manners.

"So Amy and I went and saw Governor Sterling. He sicced U.S. Marshal Hendren on them up in Globe, but meanwhile, Ernie was killed in a prison riot saving two guards' lives."

"My, my. That is bad news. Now she is dead, too." Barnabus tossed down a large shot of whiskey and said, "Ah."

Slocum stopped from eating her rich stew. "There is one more bad card in this deck. Yates hired an ambusher named Prentice who's got a needle gun and telescope. He killed that good horse I came by on last time I was through here. He's a lone wolf, and he's out there no doubt, with Yates's money in his pocket, to kill me."

"That sounds serious. You aren't drinking tonight?"

"No. Johnny and I need to hit it early on."

Barnabus nodded. "Where is Yates going?"

"I'm not certain. We're going to track him down. Oh, Hendren made us deputy U. S. marshals so we can arrest him anywhere."

"You hear that, woman?" He leaned back in the chair to look for her.

"No, what is it?" she called out.

"We've got the *federales* here with us tonight."

She came to the lit kitchen door and laughed. Then she made a bow. "Nice to have you here, *mi capitán*."

Barnabus toasted them and downed some more whiskey.

"I think you have a big job. You know what Yates will do, don't you?" Barnabus poured some more liquor in his glass.

Slocum looked up from his eating. Juanita was delivering more stew, refilling their bowls. "What?" he asked.

"If he learns you are after him, he'll leave those two gunmen behind to stop you, and he will run some more." Barnabus set his glass down hard to punctuate his warning.

"He's a crafty, mean old bastard, and he almost had this whole country for himself, except there were people like you, Amy, and them others that hung those boys. You all have made the difference. I'll drink to that." He raised his glass in another toast.

Slocum drank a short shot of whiskey with him, then thanked him. Barnabus refused his money, and then she showed Slocum and Johnny to the empty bunk room with a candle lamp.

Slocum chose a bottom bunk, and Johnny did the same. They thanked Juanita for everything, and she promised to get them up for breakfast before the sun arrived.

Slocum told the boy good night, then shed his boots and pants to get in bed. The bunk room was not cold, and there were some thick blankets on the bed. He soon fell asleep.

Two small fingers covered his lips and awoke him. In the dim light coming from the small window, he could see her shrug off a gown. Then he realized she was naked when she lifted the covers with a quiet, "Let me in with you." And he was forced to move over for her to climb into the narrow bed with him. Her smooth bare skin brushed against his, and soon her full hard breasts were nested in his chest when she moved in beside him.

"Don't worry," she whispered. "He won't wake up until noon tomorrow."

Soon, with their positioning in the narrow bed, he was on top. Her small hand reaching under him, busy kneading his dick and balls. When their mouths met, the hunger in her kisses told him she had not been with a man for a while. While the oral fire built, he gently probed her gates with his finger to make it moist enough for his entry. Shortly, she raised up and pleaded in his ear. "Oh, now, please take me away."

In her thirties, Juanita was a short woman with good-sized hard breasts and a belly, but all muscles. She made his entry easier by raising her legs higher and spreading her knees farther apart. When his turgid tool was well inside her, she grasped his arms and pulled him down on top of her. His further entry caused her to suck in her breath, and he hoped the protesting bed ropes under them didn't wake Johnny. But there was nothing else for Slocum to do but make fierce love to her tight pussy and her. And he did so until she fainted.

Seconds later, when she recovered, he closed his hand over her mouth to silence her exclamation. "Hush or we'll wake him."

"*Sí*, I am sorry. It just felt so *bueno*. Must I let you to sleep now?"

"No," he said, still pent up and wanting more. He wasn't going to let his chunky love machine leave just yet.

She squirmed to get underneath him again. "*Muy bueno*."

Aligned to go back in her, he shoved his still-hard shaft deep inside, and she sucked in her breath real hard. "Oh, that feels so good."

And it was.

18

Slocum and Johnny, full of her spicy scrambled eggs, ham, frijoles, tortillas, and topped off with some cinnamon sugar sopaipillas wrapped up in their clothes, rode north under the thick clouds that began to spit snow on them. Slocum tried to shake some of the dullness out of his head. His hangover from his torrid affair the night before with Juanita was enough—he sure was proud he hadn't drunk very much of the old man's whiskey as well.

When they reached the wagon yard at Payson, there was four to six inches of snow on everything. Hoagie Murphy ran the place, and he knew everyone. When Slocum paid him for the night, he asked Hoagie if Yates had stopped off there.

"Yates? Yeah, he's right here in town. Him and his two rannies have their horses stabled here. They're staying at the hotel. Too damn good for my bunkhouse."

"We ain't. Wonder what saloon he'll be in."

"Palace. Plays cards up there with some other big men."

Slocum thanked him. "Where's the town marshal at these days?"

"Jailhouse. Probably sleeping off a drunk."

146

"Thanks." Slocum removed the rifle from the scabbard of his saddle. He motioned for Johnny to do the same.

"You two going bear hunting?"

Slocum held his index finger to his mouth. "Sssh, I don't want the bears to hear you."

Hoagie laughed. "Good hunting out there."

They found the marshal asleep, snoring away with his boots on the desk and reared back in a spring-seat chair.

Slocum cleared his throat loud enough to wake the dead.

"Huh? What's wrong?" The lawman's beard-stubbled face turned to look concerned at the sight of their rifles. "What are you two armed for?"

"U.S. Marshal Slocum. That's Marshal Greenwood. We're here to arrest Alvin Yates on a federal warrant."

"Arrest who?"

"Alvin Yates. You know him?"

"That sawed-off banty rooster from down in the basin?"

"You know him?"

"Yeah, what did he do?"

"Falsely sent a man to prison. Harassed his neighbors to force them to move out. They have a full list of his offenses."

The man chewed on the right side of his sun-scarred lip. "You know he's got two bodyguards with him?"

"You figure they'll buck federal officers?"

"They damn sure might."

"Their names are Conroe and Morris," Slocum said.

"I never caught their names. But they ain't ordinary ranch hands."

"I have never seen them. I've only seen Yates at a distance."

"My name's Homer Frey." He planted both boots hard on the floor. "I'll back you. Try not to shoot any resident of this town. Those three don't count. Give me ten minutes or so to get me a beer and be on the far end of the bar."

"Where's the card table he'll be playing at?" Slocum asked.

"Right side. Center of the room under a wagon-wheel light. He usually sits with his back to that west wall."

"Where will the gunhands be?"

"One for sure will be standing at the bar. Yates may be expecting you."

Shaking his head warily, Frey rose, and then checked the bullets in his Colt's cylinder.

"One more thing," Slocum said. "Will Yates be sitting in a captain's chair?"

"Yeah, why?"

"They're hard to draw from for a man sitting down."

Frey agreed, put on his hat, and started to leave the office. "I'll be there, but I don't like it."

"Rather we handled it?" Slocum asked.

He shook his head and went out in the cold night.

They were alone in the office, which smelled of chewing tobacco, men's sweat, and piss. The dark iron-bar cells were empty. Slocum planned to stash Yates in one of them, and the hard asses with him if they put up a fight.

"Johnny, I know this will be a tough deal. Shoot only if you need to. I can't tell you when. But they make a wrong move, put them down."

He swallowed hard. "I understand, sir."

Slocum focused on the large ring of keys on the desk. Things could get tough over there. They better get going. Frey had had enough time to get set up.

Outside, the stars were out. The temperature had fallen. Snow crunched under their soles. They walked in the empty street the half block to the Palace. Inside, someone was playing a squeeze box and singing an Irish folk song in tenor.

Slocum stopped before the snow-caked boardwalk, between the half dozen horses hitched at the rack, and studied the double doors. The summer batwings must be tied back inside. That's what most saloon operators did in the winter.

"Take a real deep breath," he told Johnny. "There may not be much air for the next few minutes."

"I'm ready."

"Come in behind me and then slip to the left and wide of me in case they try to shoot at me."

"Yes, sir."

The door opened outward and the tenor was singing " . . . when Irish eyes are smiling—"

"Everyone sit tight," Slocum ordered, the rifle stock in his shoulder as he looked down the gun barrel at his shocked-looking target. "I'm a U. S. marshal here to arrest Alvin Yates."

From the corner of his eye, he saw Johnny move and drive the butt of his rifle in a man's midsection. Standing over him, Johnny, with his gun muzzle in the gasping man's face, said, "Don't try nothing."

Slocum held his gaze on the short man rising out of his chair at the table with hands held up. Satisfied with Yates in his sights, he stepped over and kicked away the downed man's handgun that had spilled on to the floor.

A pin could have dropped until Yates said, "You ain't no gawdamn lawman."

"The warrant I have in my pocket is for you, Alvin Yates, and I am duly sworn in to arrest you. Get over here." Slocum motioned with his rifle.

"What's your name?" Johnny asked the downed man.

"Morris—"

Yates was coming toward Slocum through the pale-faced crowd. "Where's Conroe?" Slocum demanded.

No answer. Slocum glanced down at Frey at the end of the bar.

The lawman shook his head. Conroe wasn't in there. Where the hell was he at? Not good. Slocum made Yates turn around, and took the .38-caliber six-gun out of his holster.

"Stand at the door. Try something and you're dead, do you savvy?"

"Yeah."

With his left hand, Slocum jerked Morris by his collar to his feet. "I'm holding you as an accessory." Then he turned to the customers. "Sorry to bother your evening, folks. Go back to doing what you were doing.

"Johnny, I'm walking those two down the center of the street to that jail. You take the boardwalk and watch for anything that moves. Stay in the shadows as much as you can."

"Yes, sir."

The boy had done great. How he'd seen Morris go for his gun and stopped him, Slocum would never know, but he felt lots of pride in him. Frey wouldn't be so skeptical of Johnny either from there on out.

Slocum figured the next ten minutes might be the longest his life. Where was Conroe? When he stepped out into cold night air, he decided they might soon find out. When Johnny was in place, Slocum nodded for him to go ahead. Lots of words he wanted to pile on a sixteen-year-old boy for the next three hundred feet. But this wasn't the time or place.

Snow crunched under Slocum's soles. Must be getting colder. "Halt right there," he ordered as he stood between two horses at the hitch rack. Both of his prisoners stood in the starlit, snowy street. He checked all he could see around him—the dark businesses facing the main street and the pine-top silhouettes above them.

"You ain't getting by with this," Yates said.

"Shut up." Slocum turned his ear to listen to a dog barking somewhere out behind the saloon. He didn't need any distractions from Yates. Nothing.

"Move out. No fast turns or twists. Right down the middle of the street. My finger is on the trigger and I'll cut you down before you can reach any shelter."

"I'm saying you can't—"

He jabbed Yates hard enough with the rifle's muzzle to make him stumble forward. "I said shut up."

Every nerve in his body tensed as he watched everything around them. Johnny was on the porches and boardwalk with his back to the businesses. With the rifle in his hands ready, Slocum watched Johnny quickly cross the open spaces for the next porch.

The jail was a hundred feet ahead on the left. Where was Frey? Strange the man didn't come on. He must have known they planned on putting the prisoners in his hoosegow. Then some shots shattered the night.

"Move. Move," he ordered. "Johnny, go open the jailhouse door. That might be Frey shooting."

The youth raced for the jail. Looking back over his shoulder, Slocum herded his prisoners at a jog for the same place. Something was happening or had taken place behind the Palace.

Inside, he motioned the prisoners to the cells. He picked up the keys and set down the rifle. When the two were locked inside, he turned to Johnny. "I want you to stay here and guard them. Only open the door for Frey or me. Shoot the rest. I'd turn out the lights in here, but that's up to you."

"Slocum—"

He paused in the doorway with the rifle again in his hand.

Johnny waved him on. "It's nothing. We can talk later."

"You did good tonight." Then Slocum turned, ran out, and crossed the street. On the porch of the saddle shop, he hailed a man running down the street.

"What happened?"

"They—shoot—Marshal Frey."

"Who did?"

"Some Texas cowboys. I've got to get Doc."

"Go." He hurried to the Palace and burst in the doors. The men who were crowded around the one lying on the floor parted.

Slocum knelt. "How bad is he?"

Frey looked up and winced. "Don't worry about me. I tried to take Conroe when he came back in and some ranny jumped in. I didn't know him." Frey quit talking and made a face, obviously in deep pain. Blood was coming from between his fingers where he clutched his left arm

"They ran toward the livery—"

"Take care of him." Slocum rose, and hurried outside. His soles hit the snow but he kept his balance as he ran for the wagon yard.

Half a block away in the pearl light off the snow, he saw the first rider fighting with his circling horse to get him in the street.

"Halt and throw down your guns," he ordered.

The rider threw a wild shot in his direction. *You asked for it.* Slocum was already on his knees, then took careful aim and squeezed the trigger. Black-powder smoke swept over his face, but before it momentarily blinded him, he saw the rider fly off his horse.

Slocum was on his feet. Someone else on horseback tore out of the yard, and turned his horse hard east. The pony lost his footing, went down, spilling his rider on the snow.

Slocum was there, and covered the second downed man. "Get up."

"I can't. My damn leg's broke—"

"What's your name?"

"Conroe," the man said. "I need a doctor."

The horse was already up, shaking off snow and stirrups. The first rider never moved. In his fury over the whole deal, Slocum grasped the second one by the coat collar and simply dragged him screaming on his butt through the snow toward the jail.

"Open the door, Johnny. I've got one more," he shouted.

His man stepped out on the front stoop of the jail with his rifle ready, and very efficiently checked around for anything out of place. "That all of 'em?"

"I hope to God it is."

19

His three prisoners were in irons and riding in the back of a light farm wagon that Slocum hired to haul them. They arrived in Oxbow late that next afternoon. He and Johnny sat their horses and talked as the curious began to gather around the rig.

"You run home and tell your mom that you're all right," Slocum said. "I wouldn't tell her too much. She might skin me alive for getting you in all that up there. Meet me here at sunup. Tell Star we'll be back in three or four days and relieve him. After we get these three in the Gila County jail, we can come home."

"I'll sure be back here in the morning," Johnny promised, and tore out for home.

"What's going to happen to them, Marshal?" a man asked.

Oh, he was speaking to me. Slocum about laughed. "That's for a jury to decide."

"We could save you lots of money and time."

A cold chill ran up his jaw. The man wanted to hang them. No, not on his watch. As bad as he hated that mouthy Yates for all he did to Ernie and Amy—he couldn't see him tried by rope.

153

He booted Bollie up close to the wagon and parted the onlookers. "These men are my prisoners. There will be no talk about lynching them. Any person takes that on will be tried for murder. I don't care how many there are. And you'll have to kill me first."

"Mister, you done all of us the biggest favor a man could ever ask," the tall lean man said, climbing on the wagon wheel to speak to the small crowd. "I'm going home and sleep tonight for the first time in years knowing this damn Yates and his men are out of business. They ain't going to hurt my family or me ever again."

A cheer went up, and Slocum thanked them. "It'll be a better place to live. Now, there's two more of these cruel men on the loose. One's a hired killer and rides a buckskin horse. Trust me, he's out there and a cold-blooded killer. The other one murdered Amy Branch. His name's Farnam. They're too dangerous for any of you to take by yourself. But if you see them, send word to me."

"I've seen that yellar horse—three days ago way up on Rye Creek," a man in the crowd said. "He faded into the chaparral."

"I'll be back in three to five days. You see him again, send word to Tommy Burke. I'll get it."

They locked the three prisoners in Tommy's woodshed. Tommy and three other men he promised Slocum he could count on were going to stand guard. Slocum used the saloon-keeper's bed and slept. Before dawn, he awoke, blinked his dry eyes at reality, and then combed his too-long hair back with his fingers.

Someone was out in the kitchen add-on rattling iron skillets and Dutch ovens. Slocum could smell fresh coffee. He dressed, strapped on his holster, and went over to the kitchen. The aroma of food cooking, sharp wood smoke, and the room's heat swept his face in the doorway.

A woman in her thirties reared up from stoking wood in the range and blinked at him. "You must be Slocum?"

"Yes, ma'am."

"I'm Dover Hanks's wife, Emily. He's one of your guards." She was busy fixing a cup of steaming coffee, and handed it to him.

"Thanks. Smelled all that cooking and knew Tommy wasn't doing that."

"Aw, we all look out for him. Guess Hallie Greenwood tended to you when you were bunged up. I wanted to met you then, but never got away to do it. I'm sorry about what happened to Amy. Her and Ernie were real heroes, getting you to come in and help us and all."

"Things in this basin are going to be much better, Emily. We'll get these men tried and a new sheriff in office."

"Well, thanks anyway." Emily laughed out loud with a sly grin of discovery. "I see now why Hallie didn't need any help taking care of you."

"You up already?" Tommy asked, coming in the room from the back door with a draft of cold air.

"Any problems last night?"

"Naw. Went good," he said, taking his refilled coffee cup from her.

"I hope by midnight tonight they're in the Gila County Jail."

Both men squatted on their heels out of Emily's way, sipped their coffee, and made small talk.

"Better stoke the fire in the saloon stove if you all're going to eat breakfast in there," Emily said.

"Stay here and keep Emily company," Tommy said to Slocum. "I can handle it."

"I guess, in most communities, nice women don't cook meals for the saloon bunch." Emily shrugged her shoulders under the dress. "But we've all had to lean on each other through this ordeal. It's why many of us stayed here despite Yates."

"Hey, Hallie's care got me through it, and I knew the first time I laid eyes on her that she was a ranch housewife stepping in. Lines drawn in the sand only keep apart folks that can usually help one another."

Emily nodded. "We're learning that. Learning that we can't let some bully like Yates come in here and run us off our land and ranches."

"I think it will turn out all right."

He rose, and she handed him a heaping platter of fried ham to take in to the saloon. "I'll bring the Dutch oven and we'll get started in there."

The sweet aroma of the meat filled the room. How many cold camps had he slept in overnight when he would have paid a king's ransom for a meal like this one? Damn shame he couldn't stay around for the future.

20

The horses in the team hauling the prisoners were dropping their heads in weariness and snoring in the dust. Stars pinpricked the sky. Slocum felt like he could sleep for ten years if he could find a warm place to fall down. His breath came out in clouds, and he frequently changed hands, so he could warm one of them under his blanket poncho.

Globe, wedged in between some steep mountains that were outlined against the sky, looked asleep. They stopped in front of the courthouse and the driver, Atlas Siegel, set the brake. "Whew," he said. "Those last few miles were hell for me to keep awake."

Slocum dismounted and gave Johnny his reins. "A bed will sure be appreciated."

"What time is it?" Siegel asked as Slocum unloaded the grumbling prisoners in a rattle of chains. Morris helped Conroe, who was using a crutch under one arm to hobble on his bound-up reset leg.

"It's way past my bedtime," said Slocum. "You three go up those stairs. You know where the sheriff's office is at." Slocum turned to his two. "Stable those horses and meet me back here. We'll get us a warm bed somewhere to die in."

Yawning big, Slocum herded his wards inside. He found a sleepy jailer who blinked at the sight of his hatless captives.

"Who are you?"

"Marshal Slocum here with three prisoners. Sheriff Hendren is expecting us."

"What're they charged with?" The man stood there as if that made a difference.

"You find them a cell before I come unwound. We've been on the road almost twenty-four hours. Now get them locked up. We can do the rest in the morning or afternoon."

"Yes—sir."

Slocum sighed. It couldn't go fast enough to suit him. He unlocked Morris's handcuffs and the chain that held them together.

"Slocum, I ever get a chance, I'll kill you," Yates said when Slocum went to undo his cuffs.

He looked down at the short man. "I'll just leave you in those irons tonight, you no-account sumbitch. For all you did to my friends, I should have let that crowd up there hang you. But I really wanted you to suffer working on a chain gang in Yuma."

"Fuck you."

"I wish someone would," Slocum said. Not unlocking Yates's irons, he stepped over and undid Conroe's chain. It was around his waist because of his broken leg.

When the three prisoners were locked in cells, the jailer signed a receipt for them and handed it to Slocum. "You will be back to fill out the papers?"

"When I awake."

"It's really against procedure to do this."

"I know, but it won't get you fired." He went out the door, and met an out-of-breath Johnny coming to meet him.

"Horses are watered, grained, and put up. They've got bunks at the wagon yards and a stove. Man says we can sleep there till noon."

"Good job. Let's go sleep there till noon."

"Whew. I don't know if I could be a lawman full-time after all this. You aren't one, are you?"

Slocum laughed and threw his arm over the youth's narrow shoulders as they hiked up the steep hill. "I am probably the furthest thing from a lawman you'll ever meet."

The next morning, Hendren found them. He woke Slocum, and then with his hat cocked on the back of his head, he sat on the empty bunk opposite while Slocum tried to get the cobwebs out of his brain. With his calloused hands, he scrubbed his whisker-stubbled face and wondered how long he had slept. Felt like no time.

"Do you want a job?" Hendren asked.

"Hell, no." Slocum chuckled.

"I've been by the jail. How did you get him so fast?"

"Me and Johnny were tired of eating our own cooking. No, he wasn't that far away. He had to stop and play cards in Payson. Marshal Frey got shot up there arresting the third one. And we drove hard. I hired Siegel and his wagon to transport them."

"You did fine. What about the last two, this Prentice and Farnam?"

"I expect they have flown the coop by this time. What do you need?"

"I got a wire from Prescott. My deputy Dammond thinks that Farnam is hiding down around the Crown King Mine."

"He going after him?"

"I wondered if you might consider it. You know him. He'll be tough to arrest. But you also have a good reason to want him arrested."

Slocum rose and pulled on his pants. He had lots of reasons to want that worthless sumbitch behind bars. Seated again, he pulled on his socks and then his boots. "I'll see what my partner says."

"I heard all about it," said Johnny. "Yeah, I'm ready to go help."

"Your mother would kill me."

"Hey, I did my part in Payson."

"Yes, you did. Saved my bacon. But going after Farnam is going to be different. He damn sure ain't got nothing to live for but a noose around his neck."

"What about Prentice?" Hendren asked.

"He may have quit the country. If he knows that Yates is in jail, then we've taken his meal ticket away."

"What if he has some idea about getting revenge on you?"

"Hmm." That was a notion. Slocum had to think about his last scrape with the ambusher.

It had been in Texas during the Barr-Canton Range War. More like a family feud than a range war, and Slocum'd been hooked up with Kathy Barr, Clayton Barr's widow, at the time. The Barrs and the Canton clan were killing each other off at the rate of one or two family members every few months. The patriarch of the Cantons, Antonio Canton, had hired Prentice to subtract some more Barrs.

Prentice was all set up in a barn loft to take out Florida Barr, one of the sons of Kathy's brother-in-law. Beforehand, Slocum, after hearing some gossip about Canton's plans and getting some information that he paid for, managed to slip up on Prentice in a barn.

"Put your hands high," he said, leveling his Colt at the man standing near the loft door.

"Who are you?" Prentice set his rifle down carefully

"The man who's going to stop you from shooting Florida Barr."

"How did you know I was even here?"

"I made it my business. Walk this way. No tricks." The barn loft was half empty and the hay dust was irritating Slocum's nose. He sneezed, and Prentice jumped down through the loft floor opening.

Slocum sneezed again, and then he jumped down in to the aisle below in pursuit of Prentice, hoping to get a shot at the gunman. But Prentice was already on his horse and racing away. That was the only time Slocum had had any close contact with the ambusher, and the only time that he'd seen the man's face.

"I never got another glimpse of him again after I stopped him from killing a man in Texas and he got away from me," Slocum told Hendren. "He might want revenge. I don't know."

"A lone wolf like that sure might want some. You've done it to him again. Stopped him from finishing his business." Hendren looked grim and shook his head. "I'm going to extend that marshal badge for both of you."

"Better put that extension for Star, too. He's been keeping the ranch while we ran all over. I'm certain he wants to go, too." Slocum shared a nod with the anxious Johnny.

"What do you need from me now?" Hendren asked.

"Pay Atlas Siegel for his wagon and team. Pay our livery board bill here."

"I can handle that. As my posse men, you're entitled to a dollar a day. So I'll write up a bill for seven days for all three of you."

Johnny grinned big. "Thanks for me and Star."

"Well, he was part of this, too. It's the least I can do. When are you leaving?"

"Soon as we get our money, we'll head back for Oxbow and go from there."

Hendren nodded. "It may take a day for me to get that money."

"We'll get it later." Slocum was putting on his poncho. "We better ride if we want to get back to your place by dark, Johnny. Can you pay Atlas now? I bet he wants to go home."

"I will if I have to dig the money out of my pocket."

Slocum thanked Hendren, and in fifteen minutes, he and Johnny were mounted and headed out. The sun had begun to warm up, and they pushed their ponies hard for the ferry. It was late afternoon when they finally struck the Tonto Basin Road, and long past dark when they finally reached the Greenwood Ranch.

The stock dogs barked and a light went on in the house. Star came down with his rifle in hand.

"You boys getting in late," he said to them.

"Sore-assed as hell, too," Johnny said, dropping out of the saddle. "How's it been going here?"

"I killed a lion two days ago that got a yearling colt."

"How big was he?"

"Real big. Close to two hundred, I'd guess. He was a huge tom."

Wrapped up in a shawl, Hallie came out and joined them, her breath steaming like the rest in the chilly night. "It was a large mountain lion. Wait till you see his hide. How are you two?"

"Bone tired." Then Slocum nodded with a sigh.

"No problems?" she asked.

He shook his head. "Those three're in jail."

"You two had any supper?"

"It can wait."

"He's right, Mom," Johnny said. "We left Globe mid-morning."

"Hey, I'll put up the horses," Star said. "You two head for bed."

"That's resolved. See you boys at breakfast." She walked with Slocum to the cabin. The two boys went off talking in the night.

Inside, he shed the poncho, clearing it over his head, and then discovered her standing in front of him. "I'm dirty as a pig. More whiskers than a billy goat and—"

She placed her index finger on his mouth and then hugged him. "You are an easy man to miss, Slocum."

"Could I sponge off?"

"I'd feel I was keeping you awake."

"You have any warm water on the stove?" He kissed her, and then she went to put out some in a washbasin. He toed off his boots and began to undress.

"I never thought things would get as tight as they did up

at Payson. Johnny saved my life." He elaborated on the whole thing.

Soon, she was washing him with a soapy rag, and then rinsing it out to get the soap off. Tired as he felt, the reflective heat off the fireplace and her gentle hands relaxed the ache in his back.

"He said it was exciting, arresting them," Slocum continued. "And Marshal Frey, who looked at him like he was kid when we first went into his office, never did that again. No reason for him to after we made those arrests. Boys his age were Texas Rangers fighting Comanche."

"I'm their mother, but I know both boys needed this experience. I'm so glad you're here to show them. I'm glad that we're free of Yates."

She dried him off briskly, and then rubbed her palm over his cheek. "Better shear you, too. I have some hot water for that. Sit down."

"Star mention seeing anything of that ambusher?"

Working up lather with the pig-bristle brush in the mug, she shook her head. "We were in Oxbow yesterday for a few things and a chance to show off his lion hide. It was a huge one."

She grinned big at Slocum. "That did Star good, too. Him killing that cat. Anyway, everyone was talking about Yates being gone and they're planning a celebration dance."

"When is it?"

"Saturday night. And I've got a list of ladies that want to dance with you."

He sat in a chair before the hearth, and she began peeling off his whiskers with a steady hand on the straight-edge razor, then swishing off the soap and residue in the wash pan.

"You do dance, don't you?" she asked

"Yes, ma'am."

"I'll starch a white shirt for you to wear. You and the boys' dad are about the same size and I've been sewing. I made a new vest for you. All it needs is a button, but I want you to try it on first."

"You're spoiling me."

"On purpose," she said, using her wet rag to get the remaining soap off his face.

"You know—"

"I know lots of things. Just don't tell me when." She hugged his face against the housedress and rocked him back and forth.

He closed his tired eyes and breathed in her cinnamon-lavender smell. It wouldn't be easy to leave this place or her.

21

The next day was Thursday, and Hallie let them sleep in until sunup. The wind was sharply northern, and he awoke when she came in with an armload of wood. The cold air riding on her dress tail swept into the room before she could use her butt to close it.

"Morning."

"Yeah," he said, dressing quickly. "Them boys must be ready to bust in."

"No, they respect our privacy. They won't come unless I ring the triangle."

He put on his shirt, holding his open pants up by being a little straddle-legged. "Come over. I've got a kiss for you."

With a shrug, she put down the wood, and then she walked over as he tucked the tail in. He took her in his arms and kissed her hard. "Now, you want me to ring the bell for them?"

She laughed. "Now, you may."

Her eggs were frying and the side meat sizzling in another skillet when the boys came inside and picked up cups of coffee. Making the usual morning conversation, they gathered around the fireplace while she finished breakfast.

"What are we doing today?" Star asked Slocum.

"Fixing shoes on horses. We may need to ride over to the Bradshaw Mountains and look for Farnam after Saturday night."

"What's that mean?"

"They're having a big dance in Oxbow. Your mother committed us. Who's the best farrier of the two of you?"

Johnny pointed at Star.

"Johnny, you need to ride up to the Watson Ranch and return that horse I borrowed from them. If it's all right with your mother, we need to invite them to come down here Saturday to go to the dance and stay overnight here."

"That's a good plan," Hallie said, putting the food on the table. "They never see anyone and might enjoy the dance."

"What's his name?" Johnny asked.

"Calvin Dean. She's Dana Ruth," Star said.

"Good, I can do that," Johnny said, taking some eggs off the platter and passing it on.

Star shook his head. "Bro, you get all the good deals."

"If you wasn't so damn good at horseshoeing—sorry, Mom."

Slocum had a hard time not laughing. He recalled at that age coming home from a hunting trip and letting out "sumbitch" at the table.

The day warmed some on the sunny side of the open shed where Slocum and Star worked. Bent over, working a rasp and sending black shavings in the dry horse manure-dirt mixture, was hard work. The forge sent off bitter coal smoke to heat the plates. The anvil rang as shoes were pounded into shape to fit. Holes for the nails were punched out of them and then slapped on the prepared hoof. With a short-handled hammer whacking away, the shoe soon was tacked on the hoof and the nails were cut and turned back.

It was hard, backbreaking work, with lots of whoas and scolding to keep the impatient horse's attention. Finally, they could drop the finished hoof, straighten their backs holding their hands on their hips, and walk out the cramped muscles in small circles.

Hallie finally stopped the hard work with a tray of coffee and hot cinnamon rolls. "Break time."

They washed their hands in the spring-fed horse tank and swung the hands dry.

"We're ready," Slocum said, coming across to where she had rested the tray on a manger.

"Star's like his father. Everything he does is neat," she said.

Blowing on his coffee, Star laughed. "Not that good, but I'm trying."

"I've seen his craftsmanship all over this place," said Slocum.

"No wind comes though any cracks in his buildings. His roofs never leaked. I wish I'd paid more attention now," Star said.

"It will come in time. He left you some good patterns," Slocum said.

Star nodded, and they enjoyed the mouth-watering hot sweet rolls and the coffee.

Mid-afternoon, they completed the shoeing process and fell in the hay to rest awhile.

Star sat up and chewed on a straw. "You mentioned going after those two. How far is Crown King?"

"About as far as Prescott."

"Two hard days?"

"There sure ain't no wagon road over there the way we'll go."

"Be good. See some new country. I've never been west of the Watsons."

"Been to Prescott?"

"Nope. Went to Mesa once with Dad to get some barley. They've got the widest streets I ever saw. You can turn a wagon team around in them."

"I know they planned on lots of traffic. Prescott's a booming cow town."

"Hey, that must be Johnny coming back."

Slocum had heard the horse, and Johnny wasn't wasting any time getting back. They both ran to the gate.

"What's happened, Johnny?"

"I—" He tried to catch his breath. "That sumbitch on the buckskin horse—I seen him."

"Where?"

"On the Verde crossing. I was coming home—" He dropped out of the saddle. "I looked over there in the willows and things, and saw his yellow horse. Damn. Made the hair raise on the back of my neck. Me and old Toby crossed the river like we were on fire. I—kept expecting a bullet in my back."

"You see *him*?"

Johnny shook his head. "No, just that horse."

"What're we going to do?" Star asked.

"You and I better ride up there and look around for any signs." Damn, he sure hoped that Prentice had ridden on. This made a new ball game all over again. Would they be the hunter or the hunted with Prentice?

"Oh, the Watsons said they would be here Saturday. She was sure proud we invited them." Johnny was hanging on the fence, still gathering his breath. "Nice folks."

Hallie soon joined them, and she heard the story. "You two better take bedrolls and some food along. These winter days are short."

"She's right," Slocum agreed. There wouldn't be much over three hours daylight left. "We better hold up and go early in the morning. It will give him a chance to settle down if he saw Johnny, which I am certain he did."

"My turn to go this time, little brother," said Star. "The chicken pen needs cleaning out tomorrow."

Slocum was pleased the horses were shod and ready. No telling what they'd find looking for Prentice. But he'd rather be the hunter than the hunted in this case—especially with him toting another long-range weapon. They'd get him. He should have left when the getting was good. Like Hendren said, no one knows what goes on in the head of a man like that.

They went over their saddle gear and everything. Finally, Slocum called for a nap, and the boys laughed. "Paw would have found something for us to do."

"Well, go prop up your feet and relax till supper. Johnny's got to clean the chicken pen tomorrow, and we've to got to find Prentice."

He went to the house, washed his hands and face, and knocked.

"Come in."

"I thought I better knock."

She smiled from her rocker. "I don't know why. You've seen every inch of me."

"Aw, you deserve some privacy, Hallie."

"I wasn't complaining. You know, I wonder about you."

He swung a ladder-back chair out, straddled it backward, and put his chin on the top rung. "Why is that?" he asked.

"You have no base. No attachment anywhere. You are here today and gone tomorrow, right?"

He nodded. "It's not that I don't want to stay in one place—but they'll eventually come. I know that."

She went back to sewing on the button, then tied off the thread and cut it off with her teeth. "Here, try it on for size."

He rose over the chair, took the garment, and stuck his arms in before he pulled it in place. The black-striped gray wool vest with four deep pockets fit him perfectly. "Lovely vest. Too good to wear."

"No, I made it for you to wear. Why is it too good?"

"First thing I'll do is snag it on some catclaw bush." He handed it back to her.

"Makes no difference. As long as it lasts, you'll have a small reminder of me. I think I want that. Leave an impression."

"Oh, Hallie, I am impressed with you."

She dropped her chin and shook her head. "Over those mountains out there is another woman who's gonna make a damn fool out of herself to please you."

He chuckled. Maybe she was right.

"What's so funny?"

"Your appraisal of me."

"It's not funny, it's the damn truth." Then she laughed,

too. "You bring my son back cussing and I have to laugh. He sounded like his father. Oh, hell, I've cussed again.

"Whatever you do, don't take off before Saturday night. There's too many women in the basin want to dance with you."

"Star ever speak to you about his situation with that girl?"

"No, but I could tell he wasn't over her."

"You don't get over them. They wear down eventually."

"I don't know. I've only had two men in my life. One got himself killed and the other is going to ride off. I better get supper."

He closed his eyes for a moment, and when she got up, he moved to her rocker. She fed the fireplace and went to making supper. He rocked slowly, creaking the rockers on the floor. *No, Hallie, I won't forget you that fast.*

In the morning, he and Star left before the sun even tried to come up. They'd packed some food, utensils, and bedrolls on his leggy packhorse Bob and headed west. Midday, Slocum found the tracks where the buckskin horse had been tethered in the brush above the crossing where Johnny had seen him.

Star soon picked up his tracks, and tossed his head westward. "He took Old Crooked Legs this way."

They soon were on a stock trail that led southwest. Slocum craned his neck around, not wanting to be the shooter's next victim. "Where are we going?"

"I've been to a place down here where there's water and usually grass. I'd call it an old Injun sacred place. I never stayed in there long, but it may be where he's hiding."

"Worth a try. What made you think it was sacred?" Slocum studied the skyline to their west. It was dotted with low junipers.

"There's some sweat lodges there, too. You know, they were made of sticks bound in small squares. They throw skins over them and sit in there and sweat the devil out of themselves."

Slocum laughed. "They cleanse their minds and bodies in

there. Why, a good sweat bath and some fat puppy-dog meat and you'd be a wiser man."

"Not me. You ever done that?"

Slocum nodded.

Star twisted in the saddle and looked in disbelief at him. "Damn."

"Oh, Star, you'll do lots of things in your life. Some you'll talk about, others you'll just pass and ride on."

All at once, Star began to laugh over his discovery. "What was her name?"

"Woman Who Dances with Flowers."

"I'll be a sumbitch." Star rode on, shaking his head.

Mid-afternoon, they were bellied down looking over the sacred place and studying it with his telescope.

"Here, see that lodge covered with old canvas and grass?"

Star took the brass instrument and nodded. "What do you think?"

"I have half a notion that he's in there taking a sweat bath."

Star's eyes flew open and his jaw dropped. "He's taking a sweat bath?"

"I believe he's doing it. Take your rifle and go down that way. I'll come in from this side. Be real quiet. Use cover, but we need to move in on him quickly. Remember, he's slippery and a killer."

"I know. Damn," Star swore, and shook his head in disbelief. "Let's get him."

The way off the hill proved steep, and there were lots of loose volcanic rock outcroppings to cross. Slocum caught his balance and looked real quick at the lodge. Nothing. He saw Star coming from the north.

They were in the danger area—where a shoot out with rifles could be fatal. Then, Slocum's heart beating hard under his chest, he moved softly across the dry sand—rifle ready at his hip as he closed in on the lodge.

Star was thirty feet to the other side. Slocum faced the flap. He shared a nod with his partner, and they both stood, guns cocked, as the shocked face appeared in the flap. He looked very pale-skinned. His blue eyes turned almost red with his anger.

"How did you find me?" Hands up, he emerged naked as Adam.

Slocum used his right hand to make him come to him. "You shouldn't ride crooked-legged horses. They're easy to track."

Slocum bent down and shook out Prentice's britches for concealed weapons. A jackknife and some change fell out on the ground. Satisfied, he threw them at Prentice. "Get dressed."

"What've you got planned?"

"You're lucky as hell, Prentice, this time. Me and U.S. Deputy Marshal Star Greenwood are going to take you to the Gila County Jail. Otherwise, I'd've left your carcass here for the coyotes."

"Huh?"

Slocum shook his head then reared back and drove the butt of his rifle into Prentice's stomach. His efforts spilled the naked ambusher on his ass.

Gasping for his breath, Prentice demanded, "What the hell did you do that for?"

"A damn good roan horse of mine you shot. Star, go find his horse. Sooner I get this back-shooter in jail, the better I'll feel and the less tempted I'll be to kill him with my bare hands."

Long past dark, they reached the ranch. Johnny rushed out and asked, "How did you get him?"

"We waited for him to get though taking a sweat bath," Star said, and tossed Johnny the buckskin's lead rope.

"Really?"

Slocum nodded in the starlight as he heard Hallie coming from the house, and he dismounted.

"Back already?" she asked.

"We got him, Ma," Star said.

"Wonderful. You had supper?"

"No."

"Good. I have some on the stove. Come with me." She hooked her arm in Slocum's.

"Wait," Slocum said to her. "I've got a prisoner and—"

"Your posse members can handle all that. Bring him, too," she said over her shoulder, and took Slocum with her.

"What's on your mind?" he asked, being moved along by her.

"You can chain that no-good son of a—to a tree. But I promised a dozen women you'd step on their toes Saturday night."

He bent over laughing. That was what was wrong. She thought he was cutting out to take Prentice to Globe and miss the dance.

She jerked him up. "It is not funny, big man."

"Hell, Hallie, we can chain Prentice to a wagon wheel in the snow. I don't care. We won't miss that dance."

She stopped, cupped his face in her palms, stood on her toes, and kissed him. "Thank you. Now I'll go make food for the marshals and him."

Slocum watched her, carrying her dress out of the dirt, go on to the house in the starlight and then slip inside. Quite a woman.

22

Saturday dawned, and the crew plus the dejected prisoner came for breakfast. In the middle of the meal, the dogs went to barking. Star was up and at the door. "It's Dover Hanks."

Hallie frowned. "Wonder what he wants this early."

"Is Slocum in there?" The man's voice carried and Slocum rose out of the chair.

He shook his head at Hallie. He didn't know what it was about and went outside. "Come in, Hanks. I've met Emily. Nice to meet you. What do you have?"

"A letter that the sheriff sent by messenger up here for you only."

"Thanks." He went over under the lamplight and opened it.

Dear Slocum,

There were two Fort Scott, Kansas, deputies in my office today. They were bearing a twelve-year-old murder warrant for a John Slocum. I simply told them I didn't know anyone by that name. I appreciate all you have done for the people of the Arizona Territory. While I can't offer you a pardon or protection, I wanted you to know that they are in the county and searching for you.

Thanks again, Sam Hendren
Acting Sheriff, Gila County
Arizona Territory

"Good news?" asked Hallie, who was up getting Hanks some food and coffee. "Or bad?"

"We can talk later."

"Certainly."

The obvious tension brought a silence to the room. At last, Star took the prisoner out and chained him to a pine tree. After his meal, Hanks excused himself. Slocum thanked him and walked him to the door.

"See you all at the dance," Hanks said, and rode off.

"How bad is the news?' Hallie asked Slocum on the porch. He handed her the letter.

She opened it, and then sucked in her breath. "Oh, dear God, I'm sorry."

"What is it?" Johnny asked.

"Let him read it, and Star," said Slocum. "It is none of that prisoner's business."

"Right, sir." Johnny read it, and folded it back up. "Hell, I knew it was too good to last."

"Johnny, swearing is uncalled for."

"What now? You all look like this is a funeral," Star said, returning.

"Read this and don't let Prentice know a thing," Johnny said.

Star read, and reared his head back in disbelief. "Hell, this isn't fair."

"Fair or not, catch my bobtail packhorse. I'll have to pack and ride. You two will need to take Prentice to Globe on Sunday. Any money Hendren owes me is your mother's. She fed me." He shook his head at her protest.

"Where will you go?" Johnny asked.

"I want to try and locate Farnam before I go elsewhere."

"I don't understand it." Star rapped his fingers on the back of the envelope.

"It's too long and hard to explain." He took the envelope

and gave it to Hallie. "Burn it. Prentice does not need to know about it either."

"I savvy that," Star said. "We'll take him to Globe Sunday. We'll deliver him."

"I don't doubt that. Thanks to all three of you."

"I'll be sure you have what you need in those panniers," Hallie said, and headed for the cabin to check them. He knew it was an excuse to keep them from seeing her cry.

"Well, one good thing, they all have good shoes on them," Johnny said, leading Bob up. "Me and Star want you to take Bollie. He reminds us too much of Dad for either of us to ever use him."

"If you boys are certain?"

"We're damn certain," Star said.

"All right. Watch Prentice. I'd say he's escaped more jails and more arrests than any man living. And if you don't have any other choice—kill the sumbitch."

Johnny tilted his head to the side to look at him. "I know that roan horse meant lots to you. Maybe Prentice knows he's lucky you didn't feed him to the buzzards."

"Watch him. I want to get out of here before the Watsons come. Neither they nor anyone else needs to know where I'm headed. Not that they'd do it on purpose, but a slip of the tongue is all it takes."

"Folks get the word, I guarantee they'll never know where you went."

"All right, Marshals, thanks."

Thirty minutes later, he kissed Hallie good-bye and was ready to head west with Bob in tow. It wasn't as easy a parting as he'd hoped for—damn, it never was. A woman as smooth as her—hell. He kicked some horse apples and then mounted Bollie. Bent over the saddle horn, he rode out in a long trot.

His stomach was kicking him, and his shoulders hurt where that Indian stuck a lance through him. Beyond the ranch, he caught sight of the Watsons coming, and dodged off into the junipers and hid till they were by him. Then he pushed on. Dana Ruth sitting straight-backed in the spring seat—she'd be angry he wasn't there.

He made camp that night in Bloody Basin. Sitting cross-legged at his fire, he listened to the red wolves and the less aggressive coyotes He wished for a good bottle of whiskey to smooth the edges, but he had none. He finally crawled in his blankets against the night cold. Tossing and turning, he found that sleep escaped him.

His life felt like a ruby vase dropped on the rocks. The bloody pieces all over, and many too small to ever collect into one vessel. He promised himself he'd never get that involved again with any woman—but in reality, he knew that was not going to happen.

Awakened by the night wind, he discovered he must have slept some. Then again later, he roused himself at the frosty predawn. That move only made him really regret leaving her warm bed for this situation.

No way to escape the biting cold but saddle and ride. He covered lots of country that day. The sun warmed him some, and in the late afternoon, he stopped at the Calumet Mine at the base of the towering snow-topped Bradshaws. Clu Meeker was the superintendent and they knew each other. Clu came to the office door with his lopsided grin.

"Come in here."

Slocum hitched his horses. Looked around, saw nothing unusual, and stuck out his hand. "How have you been?"

"Fine. Fine. Where you headed?" Meeker asked, taking a seat behind his paper-cluttered desk. The big man reached down in a drawer and brought out a bottle of whiskey and two glasses.

"I guess Crown King," Slocum said. "I'm looking for a man by the name of Chelsey Farnam."

"Why in the hell do you want that worthless piece of humanity?"

"He murdered a woman."

Meeker nodded. "Be careful up there. There's some snow on that mountain. You might slip and fall on your ass."

Slocum raised the half-full glass and saluted him. "I'll try my damnedest not to do that."

"Farnam has a long record of suspected murders, assaults, and extortions."

"Rapes?"

"Yes, I imagine that, too. He's dangerous."

The whiskey warmed Slocum's innards going down. "You hear anything about him?"

"No, but there's a teamster up here named Hooker who might know something. Hold on, he's down at the chutes getting loaded right now."

They downed their whiskey, and Meeker put on his heavy lined canvas coat and led the way down to where the high-grade ore was sliding out of a wooden chute into a large-wheeled wagon. The sound rumbled like thunder, and lots of dust rose.

"Hooker?" Meeker waved the big man under the wide-brimmed hat aside.

"This is Slocum. He's an old friend." The two shook hands. "He needs to know where Chelsey Farnam is at."

"He's probably upstairs in that whorehouse in King. That Molly McBee and him got something going. Probably robbing the customers that have any money left when they leave her place."

"I told him the sumbitch was worthless," Meeker said, loud enough over the noise.

Hooker agreed. "Backstabber. Why do you want him?"

"He raped and murdered a good friend of mine."

With a disgusted look on his face, Hooker shook his head. "I hope you get him."

"I will. I promise you."

"Thanks," Meeker said, and motioned for Slocum to come with him. When they were far enough away that Hooker couldn't hear him, Meeker said, "That help?"

"It did. I know where to look now."

"Hey, the day's gone," Meeker said, motioning to the sun, which was already behind the Bradshaws. "Spend the night. I know some fun women we can party with and you can ride out at dawn."

"That sounds all right. Where can I stable my horses?"

"Come with me. We've got a good stable."

"I don't want to put you out—"

"I'll handle it."

"Thanks."

His horses were put up, grained, and fed alfalfa hay in the long snug barn for the mine mules and their other animals. Meeker ordered a team and carriage hooked up and brought around.

"If you want to, you can clean up in my small room while I round out the day here."

Slocum thanked him. Meeker showed him to the room. A bed, some clothing on hangers on the wall. Sparse, but a snug place, no doubt to sleep in when Meeker had to be there overnight. An older man soon knocked, and when Slocum opened the door, he shuffled in with two pails of steaming water.

"You need anything else, sir?"

"No, but thanks."

After he shaved and sponged off, Slocum felt better sitting on the edge of the bed as the early sundown began to creep over the land.

Meeker knocked. "You ready?"

"Yes."

"The horses and carriage are here."

Slocum put on his poncho and they were off. With a nice matched high-stepping team, they went up the creek road and turned in a lane. Slocum could see in the twilight that the house ahead on the rise was a two-story brick mansion.

"This your place?" he asked, looking over the post rail fence that lined the lane.

Meeker laughed aloud. "Are you serious? I couldn't afford this place. No, this is the home of Mrs. Janis Winters, widow of the late Alexander Winters, the Arizona mining tycoon."

"I'm not dressed for this place."

"Don't get uneasy. She's used to western people, as she calls us."

"I thought we were going to raise hell with some women, not go to a tea party."

"Rest easy, my friend. You will see."

At the front of the house, a young man came and took charge of the horses and carriage. Slocum took one last look around before he followed Meeker through the tall double doors where a butler took their hats and coats, which included Slocum's poncho.

"Darling!" A woman in her early thirties, maybe younger, came across the great room dressed in a fancy green silk gown. Meeker had dragged him to the wrong place. Holy shit.

"I want you to meet my good friend Slocum."

"Oh, how nice to meet you, sir." She held out her hand and he kissed it.

"Oh, my, thank you, sir. This is so very nice. My best friend, Alicia Downing, is here visiting from the East and she will be so thrilled to meet you—Slocum, is it?"

"Yes, ma'am."

"Good. Follow me. We may have some drinks in the library and Alicia should join us very soon. Clu, my darling, how was your day?"

Slocum left them to wander around, admiring shelf after shelf of books. Some he'd read in his youth, and others he'd consumed in some cold camp hemmed in by winter. Mrs. Winters brought him a glass of wine.

"I see you have quite a collection of books, Mrs.—"

Her finger on his lips silenced him. "Janis. My friends call me that, and Slocum, don't fear, my friend Alicia is lots, I mean lots, of fun."

"I'm anxious to meet her."

"You will shortly. Clu told me you are here looking for a killer."

"Yes, I am."

"That's dangerous business, isn't it?"

"A little less than being a powder monkey in a mine."

She wet her lips. "Oh, poor Alicia."

"Why do you say that?"

"I simply worry for the poor girl," Janis said with a mischievous wink.

Alicia arrived just then. A much shorter and rounder version of her friend, Alicia was wearing a fashionable brown dress with a shawl of the same material over her shoulders. Her brown hair was piled high. Slocum imagined that the preparation of it was why it took so long for her to come downstairs.

When Janis introduced them, Alicia looked taken aback. She stuck out her hand to shake his and he did it as gently as his calloused hand could manage.

Her brown eyes flew a little more open, and she drew in a breath, "My, but you must work with your hands."

"Yes, ma'am."

"Where in the South are you from?"

"I grew up in Georgia."

"Really. I just loved the Old South." She put her hand in the crook of his arm and guided him in a nearby sitting room. "When I was a little girl, I went to visit a cousin. They had this wonderful mansion and servants, and my family lived in New York, a stinking smoky place with lazy Irish domestics." She looked enthralled by her memories.

He studied her pinched upper lip, the narrow nose, the round brown eyes, and the cleavage that showed, though she acted self-conscious about the view and kept putting a shawl over it and taking it away.

"Do you have a wife?"

"No."

He supposed it was none of his business if she had a husband. So he didn't ask. They sat side by side on the leather couch in the small study. The light from the great room shone through the half-open door, and the fireplace glowed red, radiating lots of heat.

"I am surprised some woman hasn't caught you by this time."

He switched subjects. "Do you like Arizona?"

She turned and looked up hard at him. "I am just now beginning to see why I came."

"Really?"

She put his right hand on her leg. Then she reached up with her other hand to catch his neck and bring his face down to her mouth. They kissed, and he felt her leg, which drew a warm smile on her shadowy face.

They sipped wine and kisses. Her dress was soon piled in her lap. His hands ran over her stocking-clad short, thick legs, and he felt the stiff corset that contained her.

"Oh," she moaned in a soft voice. "There is no easy way for us to go much further without a complete undressing on my part. I guess you realize that from your previous experiences with a woman thusly dressed?"

"What do you suggest?"

"That I go upstairs, take off all these undergarments, and put on a simpler gown."

"Sounds reasonable enough."

"Will you accompany me?"

"Certainly."

"Will you be shocked?"

"About what?"

"That I am not as slender as my friend Janis."

Slocum laughed and kissed her. "Lots of nice things come in different packages."

"Oh," she swooned. "You, sir, are something out of 'Leather Stockings.' And a gentleman as well."

"May I carry you upstairs?"

She put her index finger to her lips. "As heady as that would be . . . no, but you may hold my hand as we flee up there." The shawl gone, she shrugged her shoulder. "They'll know what we are doing anyway, won't they?"

"I suspect so."

"Come on." She hauled him by the hand out of the

study and across the great room. At the base of the grand staircase, he swept her up in his arms. She blushed, holding her hand over her mouth, and her brown eyes danced with stars.

"Which room?" he asked at the top of the stairs.

"The middle one."

Going in sideways, he swept her into the room and set her down, kissing her long and hard. Then she turned her back to him, and he undid the dress. She stepped out of it and laid the garment over a chair at the dressing table.

As he kissed her neck when she returned, she nestled her butt into his flank. He carefully undid the strings of the corset, and when the cups fell forward, his hands replaced them and she gasped. His mouth worked on the smooth skin of her neck as he fondled her long firm breasts until the nipples turned hard as rocks.

Soon, her nakedness was being bathed in the fire's light, and she turned to kiss him. As she squirmed against him, his manhood began to rise.

"The fireplace is so warm, let's lie on the rug," she said.

So in moments, she was on her back with her short legs spread open like a book and her arms reaching out to pull him down. He undressed in record time, and lowered himself over her. Once he was inside her, she began to moan and hunch to his thrusts. Her fingernails dug in his back, and they both made fierce love to match the fire's roaring consumption of logs. Until, at last, he came deep inside her and she collapsed.

She wouldn't let him leave, and soon she was moving against his still stiff-dick buried inside her. "Ah, what a wonderful, wonderful thing."

He nodded, and went back to work.

At some point—intermission. Food and more wine were brought up on trays by the butler and servants. Alone again, they lounged naked on the hooked rug and ate what they wanted of the beef roast, fresh sourdough bread, cow butter, and prickly pear cactus jelly. Feeding each other, and pausing for kisses, and fondling, with more wine to wash it all down.

In the predawn, Slocum got up from the large bed and looked out the window. In the driveway, the team was breathing steam and the carriage was ready. Meeker was kissing the lady of the house good-bye and he was going back to the mine—to work.

He soon disappeared in the gray light. Slocum turned back to look at the sleeping form under the covers. She'd be fine for the moment. His horses were fine at the mine stables. Might as well stay awhile. Dressed, he went downstairs. Found coffee in the kitchen, where three women worked hard in food preparation.

"Ah, I thought someone else was up in my house," Janis said.

"I missed my ride," he said, toasting her with his cup.

"Do you need to leave so soon?"

"No."

"Good, bring your coffee. Tell Helena what you wish for breakfast and she'll fix it while we visit."

Janis took him into the study where a small table and two chairs were set up to absorb the fireplace's heat. She was dressed in a housecoat with ruffles down the front. It was made of fancy silk with orange and green Chinese patterns.

"I am so glad you and my friend entertained yourselves so well. Did she tell you why she is here?"

"No."

Janis searched around to be certain they were alone. "Bless her heart. Her sneaky husband left this country for England with another woman. Oh, dear, it was such a big scandal. So she came out here to hide from the newspaper reporters and all their friends. You understand?" Janis put her hand on his arm across the table. "The real gem of the evening was your gallant act of carrying her upstairs."

"Good."

"You know she is fabulously rich?"

"That doesn't matter."

Janis's blue eyes sparkled, and then she paused for a moment. "No, you don't care, do you?"

"No."

"You know you could marry her and be rich and do whatever you want to do?"

"I do that now."

She threw back her head and laughed openly. "I believe you do, Slocum. I really believe you do."

23

A week later, with the double-barrel shotgun in his hands, snow crunched under his new lace-up boots. Ahead, in some tall pines facing the snowy street, was the two-story saloon and whorehouse that Crown King boasted about. He wore the heavy felt-lined canvas coat and the fur hat that Alicia had insisted he wear so he didn't freeze any part of his body.

A window opened upstairs, and a man stuck his head and a pistol out. "That you, Slocum?"

"It's me all right, Farnam."

"I heard you was looking for me. Well, you sonofabitch, you found me. Now what're you going to do about it?"

"You hear that I was going to kill you for what you did to Amy Branch?"

"I didn't do anything to her. Who's she?"

"That's a damn lie. You raped her and then you cut her throat and then you buried her in a shallow grave up in Bloody Basin."

"I never—"

"Bullshit. I dug her up. I saw what you did to her, and I reburied her—you worthless bastard."

"Take this." Farnam's six-gun failed to fire, and the hammer fell with a dull click.

Slocum drew the twelve-gauge to his shoulder and blasted the man, window and all. Farnam fell back inside screaming. Slocum began to run. The only way down from up there was a staircase on the south side of the building. On the move, he ejected the empty metallic shell and reloaded the left barrel. The shotgun clicked shut and the left hammer was cocked.

He could hear Farnam upstairs raging at the top of his lungs how he'd kill Slocum. Slocum slid to a stop in front of the building where he could look up that flight of stairs. He raised the scattergun, ready to send the worthless piece of shit to kingdom come.

Farnam burst out the side door and made one wild shot with his black-powder pistol. Slocum's buckshot struck him in the chest and staggered him backward. But he recovered, and tried to aim again at Slocum, who was standing in the street.

He never got the shot off. The twelve-gauge roared and blasted his face away. He came tumbling down the stairs head over heels.

"Don't shoot. Don't shoot!" A fat woman in a silk dress came rushing out on the top flight and, holding one hand out, hurried down the stairs. "Oh, dear God, you've kilt him!"

"Good." Slocum ejected the empty casings and snapped the gun barrels shut.

Coming down the street, driving the high-stepping horse in front of the two-person sleigh, sat Alicia, dressed in furs and handling the horse very well. She drew up beside him.

"Your work is over here, I presume?"

He put the shotgun in the back and nodded as he climbed in beside her. "Yes, ma'am. I think we can go back to Prescott now."

She smiled, put the buffalo robe over his lap, and acting excited, clutched his arm. "I'm ready to go back there."

Slocum clucked to the horse and turned him around in the street, the steel gliders riding smoothly on the packed snow. He'd never driven a rig like this in his entire life. But earlier that morning back in Prescott, Alicia—Mrs. Downing—had insisted they take it up to Crown King so he could find Farnam.

He sat back and enjoyed driving the fine-gaited horse. Who was he to argue?

Watch for

SLOCUM AND THE BACKSHOOTERS

371st novel in the exciting SLOCUM series
from Jove

Coming in January!